ORION
RISES

BOOK TWO OF THE STAR SCAVENGER SERIES

G J OGDEN

This novel is entirely a work of fiction. The
names, characters and incidents portrayed in it
are the work of the author's imagination. Any
resemblance to actual persons, living or dead,
events or localities is entirely coincidental.

ISBN-13: 978-1-9160426-8-1

Cover design by Grady Earls
Editing by S L Ogden

www.ogdenmedia.net

THE STAR
SCAVENGER SERIES

One decision can change the course of an entire civilization. One discovery can change your life...

READ THE OTHER BOOKS IN THE SERIES:

- Guardian Outcast
- Orion Rises
- Goliath Emergent
- Union's End
- The Last Revocater

ACKNOWLEDGEMENTS

Thanks to Sarah for her work assessing and editing this novel, and to those who subscribed to my newsletters and provided such valuable feedback.

And thanks, as always, to anyone who is reading this. It means a lot. If you enjoyed it, please help by leaving a review on Amazon and Goodreads to let other potential readers know what you think!

If you'd like updates on future novels by G J Ogden, please consider subscribing to the mailing list. Your details will be used to notify subscribers about upcoming books from this author, in addition to a hand-selected mix of book offers and giveaways from similar SFF authors.

Subscribe for updates:
http://subscribe.ogdenmedia.net

Other series by G J Ogden

- The Planetsider Trilogy
- The Contingency War Series

PROLOGUE

A thousand stars had died in the time that the great ship, Goliath, had slept. With its crystal destroyed, it remained lost in the galactic center, drifting blindly through empty space. It was not organic, unlike the corporeals that had created it, yet it was alive. The passage of the centuries had not decayed its hulking, metal shell, or caused its internal components to corrode and deteriorate. Its mind, inorganic but sentient, had remained keen and focused. And with each passing century it had grown ever more vengeful.

Though it was artificial in nature, the great ship had still experienced the passage of time in the same, linear fashion as any other life form. Because of this it had experienced loneliness on a scale beyond imagining. Over thousands of years this loneliness had twisted into bitterness and resentment, and finally calcified into a ruthless

1

determination. A determination to finish what it had started millennia ago. A task that the last Revocater had prevented it from completing.

It could not feel pain, but the knowledge that it had come so close to fulfilling its self-appointed task had weighed on its consciousness for so long that it was agony in all but name. Only one planet had remained – one out of thousands it had already cleansed. The planet was in system 5118208. Eight planets, five dwarf planets and a single yellow star. The third planet was all that had stood between Goliath and the completion of its task. It could not rest until this planet was sterilized of the organic beings that inhabited it. Only then would the galaxy finely be saved.

However, the last Revocater vessel, sent by the corporeals before their cleansing, had interfered. The Revocater's brethren had all fallen to the great ship's superior might, smashed like tombstones into the planets they had desperately tried to protect. But with its dying act, the last Revocater had cast a portal so massive that it had even enveloped the great ship itself. The effort and energy necessary for such a feat had shattered its crystal, destroying any hope of it navigating a path to system 5118208. At least the last Revocater had perished in the process, ripped apart by the act of projecting such a powerful gateway.

Now the great ship's time had come again. Its patience had been rewarded. A signal had penetrated the vast depths of space, lighting up the portals like road signs, pointing the way back.

This time the Revocaters were all gone and would not be able to stand in its way. This time, it would descend upon the third planet of system 5118208 and sterilize it, cleansing it of the dangerous organics that inhabited the surface. Then the threat from the corporeals would be over. Then – and only then – could Goliath rest.

The great ship engaged its engines for the first time in thousands of years. They were engines that propelled it with the power of a star; power that it would soon bring to bear on system 5118208.

CHAPTER 1

Hudson Powell detoured sharply off Third Street and walked another full block out of his way. The few times he'd quickly glanced over his shoulder had been enough to confirm his suspicions. Either the guy behind him really enjoyed strolling around San Francisco, or Hudson was being followed.

There had been a time not all that long ago when Hudson wouldn't have even noticed. However, since people had tried to kill him at least four times in the past week alone, it was hard not to feel a little paranoid.

Hudson had chosen to walk from his hotel in the Mission District all the way into Bayview. This was partly because the surface taxis didn't accept hardbucks, which was the only currency he had. However, it was mainly because he'd woken up early with the remnants of a hangover from the

4

potent liquor he had consumed the night before, in a bar a few blocks away. The stodgy breakfast the hotel had served up hadn't quite cured his alcohol-induced ills, but the long walk into Bayview had done the job. Now he had another headache to contend with. Specifically, the question of who the hell was tailing him, and why.

Hudson thought back to the previous day, which had been one of the occasions when someone had tried to kill him. Two people, in fact. First, Cutler Wendell, the relic hunter thug hired by Hudson's former RGF training officer, Logan Griff, had tried and failed. Hudson had slugged him with a copper tube, ringing his empty head like a bell. This had led to another intense interaction with Tory Bellona, Cutler's seemingly reluctant partner in crime. She was a relic hunter mercenary and a woman who had both terrified and beguiled Hudson in equal measure. She'd let him live as payback for Hudson having aided her in the alien wreck on Brahms Three, but only after forcing Hudson to shoot her first. The crazy thing was, that hadn't even been the most insane thing that had happened to Hudson in the last week.

Then there had been the botched robbery attempt by the black-market relic dealer. This had taken place in the Antiques and Curiosity Shoppe, not far from where Hudson was walking now. Perhaps being zapped with his own stun weapon had left a bitter taste in the pompous man's mouth, as well as a nasty burn to his chest. Given that Cutler and Tory had already departed Earth in their ship, Hudson reckoned the odds were good that the crooked dealer was behind his current tail. How he'd managed to find him was the question, and it was one Hudson intended to get a swift answer to.

Hudson reached a junction in the street and saw an opportunity to slip off the path and prepare his ambush. As he lay in wait, he noticed that the street was ironically called Hudson Avenue. Sure enough, the thud of footsteps behind him began to quicken and the man raced past, before stopping on the corner and cursing into the morning air. He'd evidently thought Hudson had slipped his tail, which was true. However, Hudson had no intention of simply letting the man walk away. Springing up out of cover, Hudson grabbed the man around the neck and wrestled him off the street into the overgrown patch of trees and shrubs where Hudson had hidden. The man struggled, kicking his legs and flailing his arms, but Hudson's grip around his neck prevented him from crying out. Then Hudson drove an elbow deep into the man's gut, robbing him of breath. He then brutally twisted his arm into a lock and pressed his knee to the man's neck. If this had been a professional wrestling match, Hudson would have had a win by submission hold in less than ten seconds.

"Mind telling me who the hell you are?" growled Hudson, as the man gurgled beneath his weight, "and why you're following me?" Hudson released some of the pressure on the man's neck from his knee, but kept his arm tightly locked.

"I saw the job on the board!" the man blurted out, struggling from the pain. "Cortland posted your image and description. Said you'd robbed him..."

"Who the hell is Cortland?" said Hudson, while tightening the arm lock a little, causing the man to squeal some more. "Is that even a real name?"

"The owner of the Antiques and Curiosity Shoppe!" the man gasped. He had raced through the words since most of his breath was taken up with a variety of different anguished groans.

Hudson smiled, glad that the vast quantities of whiskey he'd consumed over the past few days hadn't dulled his senses and intuition. He'd never gotten the name of the black-market dealer who'd assessed the mysterious alien crystal, and then botched an attempt to steal it. *Cortland...* thought Hudson, as he patted the crystal, which was still safely hidden inside his leather jacket. *That name sounds suitably pompous...*

He'd inherited the crystal from Ericka Reach. She had been the relic hunter whom he'd had a brief but thrilling liaison with on Brahms Three, before Griff had killed her. It was the catalyst that had caused Hudson to get ousted from the RGF and end up back on Earth, with Griff still lusting for revenge. Hudson had cost Griff a big score, and put him in debt with Chief Inspector Jane Wash. It was a debt that Griff intended to claim in blood.

The black-market dealer, Cortland, had offered Hudson four hundred thousand credits to buy the crystal, but he'd refused. There was something about the unique alien relic that was more intoxicating than whiskey. And, like a drug, Hudson had found himself unable to part with it. He wanted to discover its secrets, and learn if there were more crystals like it. To this end, Hudson had been on his way to a used ship lot in Hunter's Point. He'd intended to buy a suitable vessel to start his own relic hunting career, but then he'd spotted the man tailing him.

"So, what's the deal?" he asked the man, who was still squirming on the grass beneath him. "Did Cortland hire you to kill me?"

"No!" said the man, almost indignantly. "He just wanted me to pick your pockets for some weird item of jewelry. Said you'd stolen something from him and he wanted it back. For obvious reasons, he couldn't go to the police, so he posted your description on the dark web dealer board, offering a reward."

"How much?" asked Hudson, out of curiosity for what the 'bounty' on him was. He felt a little like Billy the Kid, finding a 'Wanted' poster of himself on the town notice board.

"Two thousand," squawked the man, "paid in hardbucks."

Hudson couldn't help but feel a little offended. He'd hoped for a least five figures. "Is that all? What a stingy bastard."

The man squealed and yelped some more, before catching his breath for long enough to blurt out, "Please let me go, I'll stop following you!"

"I'll let you go," Hudson began, and the man's pained expression showed a slight hint of relief. Then Hudson added, more darkly, "but then you're going to take me to Cortland."

"Why would I do that?" the man yelped.

"Because we clearly have business to settle," said Hudson, lifting the man to his feet, but maintaining the arm bar. "And I have enough people on my ass as it is."

"If he sees you, he won't open the door."

"That's why you're not going to let on that I'm hiding just out of sight," replied Hudson. He could see the man was about to protest again, and so quickly added, "If you do this, I'll see to it that you get paid."

This seemed to instantly change the dynamic between the two men. Instead of being scared and in pain, the man was now intrigued and in pain.

"You'll get me the two thousand?" the man asked. Hudson had eased off the hold enough for the words to sound less strained.

"I'll get you the hardbucks," Hudson confirmed. "You just have to get me inside."

The man stopped struggling and Hudson returned the gesture by releasing his arm. He tried to shake away the stiffness, but his expression still looked pained.

"You're not going to... you know..." he began, uncertainly.

"I'm not going to kill him, no," said Hudson, finishing the man's sentence.

The man smiled, clearly relieved. "Then you have a deal, Mr. Powell."

Hudson grabbed the man's hand again, which initially made him tense up, as if he was expecting Hudson to wrestle him to the ground once more. But instead of inflicting pain, Hudson simply shook his hand.

"Call me Hudson," he said, smiling, but then he added, completely deadpan, "and don't try anything stupid, or next time, I'll pull this arm off and choke you with it."

The man's eyes widened and the smile was wiped from his face. Hudson hadn't been serious, but if he was going to become a relic hunter, he'd have to get used to being more ruthless, or at least acting that way. And judging from the alarmed look on the man's face, Hudson guessed he had sounded pretty convincing.

CHAPTER 2

Hudson huddled down against the outside wall of the Antiques and Curiosity Shoppe and waited for the door to buzz open. He heard the lock click and then pounced. Barging past the man who had been tailing him, Hudson burst inside. He immediately locked eyes with Cortland, the black-market dealer who had hired the pickpocket to rob him. The dealer froze like a rabbit in headlights as Hudson strode towards him. Panicked, Cortland fumbled beneath the counter for his stun pistol, but Hudson angrily slapped it away. Adrenalin was surging through his veins now, and he felt invincible. Grabbing the dealer by the lapels of his burgundy satin jacket, Hudson dragged him over the countertop and dumped him unceremoniously on the floor.

While this was happening, the man whom Cortland had enticed into pickpocketing Hudson anxiously entered the store. He was now standing awkwardly in front of the door with his hands by his stomach.

"Don't kill me, please don't kill me!" blabbed Cortland as Hudson stepped over the top of him, fists clenched. "I'm sorry, it was a mistake, I admit it!"

Hudson reached down and hauled Cortland to his feet, again using his flamboyant jacket for leverage. He then slammed him up against the wall, like a cop roughing up a crook in an old-fashioned movie. A few loose trinkets wobbled on the shelves behind him and then fell to the floor, smashing into tiny pieces.

"I'm not going to kill you," said Hudson, glowering at Cortland. His tough-guy act was just that – an act – but his blood was still pumping, and he couldn't deny that the rush was exhilarating. "Providing you agree to one of my offers."

Cortland seemed to be excited by the prospect of a deal. Either that, or he was merely excited by the prospect of not being murdered, Hudson couldn't be sure which. "Deal, yes, let's do a deal!" the bald dealer said, smiling nervously.

Hudson backed away to the counter and reached over the top. He felt around and then pressed the button underneath the left side to lock the door and tint the store window black. The clunk of the lock and the darkening glass seemed to make both Cortland and the pickpocket even more anxious. Then Hudson recovered the stun pistol that he'd slapped out of Cortland's hand earlier. It was the same pistol he'd shot Cortland with the day before, the first time he had tried to swindle him. The dealer did not appear happy to see it once again in Hudson's possession. Hudson knew that the memory of being shocked by it would still be raw, and so made sure Cortland got a good look at the weapon.

"I'm going to offer you two choices," said Hudson, wafting the pistol around like an orchestra conductor's baton. "The first offer is that I shoot you with this again," Hudson continued, as he tapped the stun pistol. He then wafted it back in Cortland's general direction, making the dealer clench up as if he were on a rollercoaster. "And then I rob your shop and tip off the SFPD about your little illegal side operation." Hudson paused for effect while deal one sank in, before adding, "How do you like that proposal, Mr. Cortland?"

The dealer frowned, before timidly answering, "Well... I should say that I don't like it very much..."

Hudson smiled; he was actually starting to enjoy himself. "Here's offer two then," he added, while waving the stun pistol at the pickpocket. This made the nervous man recoil, as if someone had popped a balloon next to his ear. "You pay the ham-fisted highwayman, here, the two thousand reward you promised on the dark web." This instantly made both Cortland and the pickpocket adopt confused frowns. "And then you delete your entry about me on the black-market dealer board and swear never to go up against me again." Hudson left another pause for effect, and then delivered his punchline, "In return, I'll sell you a high-grade alien CPU shard. I'll even give you a good price, by way of apology for zapping you in the chest."

"And for stealing my money..." Cortland added, clearly still resentful.

"You deserved that," Hudson hit back, "in fact, you deserved both. But the price I'll accept for the shard will more than compensate you for that minor loss."

The lines on Cortland's brow were now furrowed so deeply that Hudson could have sown seeds in them.

"Offer two would appear to be somewhat more palatable..." Cortland said, with more of his usual eloquence. "Though I must confess, I don't quite understand why you would make me such a bargain, under the circumstances." Then he hastily added, "Not that I am ungrateful for the offer, not at all."

This question forced Hudson to think. *Why am I offering this guy a deal?* he asked himself. *He's a crook and a swindler, no better than Logan Griff.* Hudson's grip tightened around the handle of the stun pistol. Just the mere thought of Griff made his blood pressure soar. It was then that he realized part of the reason why he was giving Cortland a pass. The crooked dealer may have tried to rip him off, but zapping him and then stealing back his money hadn't sat well with Hudson. He had been a little drunk when the confrontation had occurred, and in the cold (sober) light of day, he'd regretted it. Despite Hudson's initial curiosity at the bounty Cortland had placed on his head, he wasn't an outlaw and had no desire to be one. And even if becoming a relic hunter would require a certain level of rule bending, he'd rather die than end up like Griff or Wash. Or, for that matter, Cortland.

"You're right, I should kill you for being a dirty, double-crossing swindler," Hudson replied, with feeling. And though Cortland appeared indignant at the slanderous insult, the looming threat of being zapped again meant that he didn't protest. "But I did also shoot you and take back money you actually earned. So, I want to make us square."

Cortland appeared intrigued by the response and pondered his answer for a few seconds, before returning an acquiescent little shrug. "Very well, Mr. Powell, I accept your offer."

Hudson raised the stun pistol again, this time aiming it directly at Cortland's chest. This had the effect of stiffening him up like a plank. "Though, if I get even a whiff that you've gone back on the deal, I promise you I won't be so charitable," Hudson added, maintaining his tough-guy act.

Cortland held up his hands, "Believe me, Mr. Powell, I have no such intention. Don't take this the wrong way, but I'll be very glad if I never see you again."

Hudson smiled and then lowered the taser pistol. "The feeling is very much mutual, Mr. Cortland."

Without the coercive influence of a weapon being pointed at his chest, Cortland seemed to relax. His attention was then turned to the man who was still standing anxiously by the door. "There is one aspect that confuses me, however," he began, glowering at the bystander. "Why should I still pay this useless gentleman two thousand hardbucks? He resolutely failed at the task!"

The pickpocket's cheeks flushed red and he stared at the ground, looking downtrodden.

Hudson laughed, "Call it a broker's fee. He did, after all, bring us together so that we could come to this little arrangement. Besides, like I said, you'll still come out of this way better off than you started. We all do. Everybody wins."

Cortland considered this for a moment, before giving another grudging shrug of acceptance. "Very well," he said, adding an elaborate sigh for effect. "It appears that I have little choice."

Hudson reached into the compartment inside his leather jacket and removed the alien CPU shard, before placing it gently on the counter top. "Good. Now that's all settled, shall we get down to business?"

CHAPTER 3

A gentle breeze carried in from across the bay and Hudson closed his eyes, allowing it to wash over him. It felt as fresh and as crisp as a Sonoma Valley Chardonnay, and was the perfect accompaniment to the warm Californian sun.

Even better, the final remnants of his hangover were gone. *It's amazing how quickly a person's fortunes can change...* Hudson mused, as he strolled towards Hunter's Point. Yesterday, he was jobless, homeless and had only a few hardbucks to his name. Now, thanks to his new tough-talking relic hunter grit and determination, he had one hundred and fifty thousand credits. Even better, there was no-one trying to kill him – at least for the time being.

His upbeat mood took a knock as he caught sight of the rusted iron gates of 'Swinsler's Shipyard'. The proprietor of the bar where he'd been

17

drinking the night before had pointed out that it was having a sale. But on first impressions, it certainly didn't look like a place where he could buy a ship. Or at least not a ship that was capable of any form of sustained flight.

Refusing to be deterred, Hudson pushed through the gate, which screeched like a demented banshee as he did so, and entered the main forecourt. There were certainly ships inside, but each one looked like it had already been stripped down for parts. *This isn't a shipyard, it's a damn boneyard...* Hudson realized.

He was about to turn around and leave when a nasal-sounding voice startled him. A moment of dread-fear gripped Hudson as he initially expected to see Chief Inspector Wash standing behind him. However, when he spun around, he instead saw a short, yellow-haired man wearing thin, circular glasses. He must have been no more than five feet tall, and wore a bright yellow, knitted jersey with cream slacks. This made him look like a corn cob. Hudson had to force himself not to laugh out loud as the image took root in the sillier part of his mind. But the effort of forcing his mouth to remain shut resulted in Hudson grimacing as if he were desperately trying to hold in a fart.

"Are you okay?" asked the nasally man. "You look a little uncomfortable."

Hudson thumped his chest and barked out a succession of short coughs, which he kept up until he was certain the potential for giggles had gone. "Sorry, I must have swallowed a bee," said Hudson, but then grimaced again at the utter ridiculousness of this statement.

"A bee, you say?" asked the man, looking at Hudson as if he'd just escaped from a lunatic's asylum. "Would you, erm, like some water?"

"No, no, I'll be fine," said Hudson, thumping his chest a little more. Then he rapidly changed the subject to deflect from his embarrassment. "I'm actually here looking for a ship. I saw in the epaper that you had a sale on."

This seemed to flip a switch in the man's brain, and he instantly developed an oily smile. "Wonderful news!" he said, rubbing his hands together. "I only have a few left – business has been booming and my ships are in demand. If you'll come this way, Mr...?"

Hudson gave him his name and then followed behind the proprietor of the shipyard. Swinsler led him past the carcasses of long-dead ships and through another gate into a separate part of the forecourt. Inside were five ships, arranged in a wide semicircle with the noses all pointing to the center where Hudson and Swinsler were now standing. They ranged from a small, two-person shuttle that was really only good for courier runs to Earth-orbiting stations, to a mid-sized transport. The latter took up a full third of the yard. Hudson knew such a ship had great cargo potential, but there was also no chance he could crew it by himself.

He walked up to a YV-131 light freighter, a ship he'd flown before and knew well. It was reliable, tough as old leather and, importantly, it could be operated by one person.

"How much for the one three one?" asked Hudson, glancing back at Swinsler, who was still rubbing his hands together.

"Oh, a fine ship, one of my best," Swinsler began, and Hudson again had to force himself to contain his emotions, though this time it was due to exasperation, rather than the giggles. He'd heard this sort of oily sales patter a thousand times before, but though it was a game he was tired of playing, he also knew it was necessary. "Lots of interest in this one. In fact, I have an appointment for someone to view it later today," Swinsler went on, sticking to his script.

Hudson gave a disinterested sniff, "Looks a bit tired, if you ask me," he replied, "but you may as well tell me a price."

Swinsler didn't react to Hudson's lack of enthusiasm and simply stated, "A bargain at nine hundred, even. I expect it to sell within the week, so if you are interested, I'd suggest you move quickly."

Hudson's mouth went dry and he forced down what little saliva remained, before replying, "Seems a bit pricey; I'll give it some thought." It was the truest test of his poker face that he'd had for some time, and he wasn't convinced that he'd pulled off the act, but Swinsler gave nothing away.

"Of course, take your time," the salesman said, before looking behind and noticing that another person had entered the forecourt. "I'll leave you to browse, and send over my assistant to answer any further questions."

"Sure, thanks," said Hudson, smiling amiably, though inside it felt like his world had just fallen apart. It was like Swinsler had reached into his heart, pulled out his deepest desire and crushed it in front of his very eyes. *Nine hundred thousand...* he repeated to himself. Admittedly, it had been some time since he'd checked the price of starships, but he'd completely misjudged how much it would cost to get one. The YT-131 was a good ship, but even after bartering, Hudson could never get close to the asking price. Even the tiny shuttle, which was only about twice the size of a taxi flyer, would be barely within his budget.

Hudson's head bowed and his eyes fell to the floor. He may as well have been broke for all the use his one hundred and fifty thousand credits was. His dream of becoming a relic hunter had died before it had even got off the ground.

"You're not thinking of buying that piece of crap, are you?"

Hudson spun around to see a young woman standing behind him. She was wearing dirty, blue grey coveralls that matched her striking blue-streaked hair, which was pulled back into a neat ponytail. She was studying Hudson with interest, as if he were an art model that she was about to paint. Her hands were shoved through slits in the sides of the coveralls, presumably into the pockets of whatever she was wearing underneath.

"Which piece of crap, exactly?" asked Hudson. He hadn't intended it as a joke, but the answer seemed to amuse the woman nonetheless.

"The one three one," she replied pointing to the ship Hudson had enquired about earlier. "Sure, she looks okay, but trust me, that thing has more miles on it than Voyager One."

Hudson laughed, "So you're a connoisseur of fine ships, I take it?" Then he noticed that there was a patch sewn onto the chest pocket of the woman's coveralls. It was a small, round logo with the words, 'Royal Air Force' stitched alongside. He frowned, "Is that who you're here buying on behalf of?" he said, pointing to the logo. "Who the hell is 'Royal Air Force', anyway?"

The woman rolled her eyes, "So, you don't know crap about ships *or* history. Swinsler's going to have a field day with you."

"Hey, I know my ships," Hudson hit back, feeling suddenly under attack from the stranger who had rudely interrupted him, "and I've likely been flying crates like these since before you were even born. How old are you, anyway? Sixteen, seventeen?"

"Old enough to know that you're about to get ripped off."

Hudson was beginning to wonder if he had a sign on his forehead saying, 'Hi, my name is Hudson, please insult and denigrate me!', because it seemed to be the default reaction of everyone who met him. However, the woman's choice of words had goaded him; he'd had enough of being ripped off.

"Okay, smart ass, which one would you choose? I'll allow you to regale me with your sage wisdom, before you go back to school, or wherever you've bunked off from."

The woman pulled her hands out from the slits in the coveralls and folded them in front of her chest, matching Hudson's defensive posture. "I wouldn't buy any of them. But, if you're too pig-headed and stubborn to take the advice of a *girl*, it's your funeral."

The woman turned on her heels and was about to leave, but she had piqued Hudson's interest enough to make him take the bait.

"Okay, okay, you've got my attention," he said, holding up his hands, "and I'm sorry for being snippy. I've had a hard few days, which has included me getting 'ripped off' as you put it." The woman stopped and turned around again, but her arms were still folded. "How do you know that none of these are worth buying, anyway?" Hudson asked, with genuine interest.

The corners of the woman's mouth turned up, "Because I'm the one that had to fix them and cobble them back together."

CHAPTER 4

The wicked smirk on the young mechanic's face was infectious, and Hudson found himself grinning back. He'd come across a wide variety of sales tactics in his many years flying around the galaxy, but openly admitting your stock was junk was a new one to him.

"I guess that's why Swinsler does the talking," said Hudson, "I doubt you make many sales with a pitch like that."

"You mean being honest?" shrugged the woman, before shoving her hands back through the slits in her coveralls.

Hudson nodded, "You'd be surprised how rare it is to find an honest person these days."

"Believe me, I wouldn't."

Hudson smiled again and stepped towards the woman, stretching out his hand. "Hudson Powell, pleased to meet you."

"Liberty Devan," the woman replied, taking Hudson's hand and leaving an oily smear on his palm. "Sorry about that," she said, as Hudson brushed his palms together, trying to remove some of the grime. "Occupational hazard."

"Don't worry, I'm used to getting my hands dirty," said Hudson. "So, what's your story? How did you end up here, fixing up old wrecks for Swinsler and then warning his customers not to buy them?"

"Just lucky, I guess," replied Liberty, with a lazy shrug.

"I mean it, I'm interested," Hudson persisted. Then he looked back at the row of five ships. Even if what she'd said was true about them being old jalopies, it was still some feat to fix up a fleet of starships on your own. "With handiwork like that, you'd could easily get a position with the CET or one of the commercial fleet operators."

"Did you miss the part where I said they were all junk?" said Liberty, maintaining her default standoffishness.

Hudson regarded Liberty for a moment. He didn't buy her 'not bothered' act for a second. The one three one may have done more mileage than Swinsler would admit, but Hudson could clearly see it had been fixed up well. Hudson may not have been a great mechanic himself, but he was a good judge of character. And he could tell that

Liberty Devan was the polar opposite of her oily boss.

"No, but unless I've deeply misjudged you, I don't reckon you'd let Swinsler sell them if you weren't confident that they were space worthy," said Hudson. "If one of them did crash and burn, you'd know it was on you."

Liberty studied him again for a few moments, before pressing her lips into a pout, "Fine, you got me. They're all good enough to fly," she admitted, but then hastily added, "but they're still junk. Best I could do, though."

Hudson shrugged, "To tell the truth, I can't afford any of them, anyway, so it's a moot point. I might get close to a deal on that little shuttle, but it's no good for what I need."

Liberty's pencil-line eyebrows rose up and the pout returned. "So, what's your story, Hudson Powell? What do you need a ship for?" However, before Hudson could answer, she added, excitedly, "No, don't tell me – let me guess. I like this game." She began to stroll off towards the rear of the boneyard, beckoning Hudson to follow with a roguish nod of her head. "Okay, so here goes... Your wife left you for a ruggedly handsome starliner pilot with a perfect smile and a six-pack. So, you're buying a ship out of some midlife crisis act of rebellion, to show her what she's missing?"

"What? No!" Hudson scoffed. "Hell, have you got any more clichés hidden inside that boiler suit?"

27

Liberty smiled, "Okay then, so how about this... You're an aging, jaded college art professor, searching for adventure in the outer portal worlds, before he gets too old."

"Where the hell do you get, 'college art professor' from?" Hudson replied, indignantly. "And what do you mean old?!"

"What, you're annoyed that I think you look intelligent?" Liberty hit back. "And the leather jacket sort of says 'art professor' to me. Or maybe music? Anyways, you've got to be forty, right?"

"Wow, you really are a charmer, aren't you?" said Hudson, wide-eyed. "With people skills like those, I'm beginning to understand why you're stuck here fixing up old wrecks."

Liberty rolled her eyes, then led Hudson around a corner before stopping in front of a ship. Unlike the wrecks they'd just walked past, which had all been dissected for parts to varying degrees, this one looked fully intact, if a little rough around the edges. Hudson took a pace back to take it in fully, then smiled because he knew exactly what it was.

"That's a VCX-110 light courier runner," he said, after blowing out a low whistle. "Man, that's a good ship."

Liberty's face lit up at Hudson's enthusiasm for the ship, as if he'd just shown appreciation for her pet dog. "It's my own personal project. I love this ship, and one day it's going to be mine."

"You'd better hope Swinsler doesn't sell it," said Hudson, "a ship like this should be in demand. I used to fly these beauties from Earth all the way out to Chimera Four in the OPW territories. They never let me down once."

"Except she doesn't fly; she's crippled," replied Liberty. "That's why she's back here, till I manage to fix her up, anyway. Swinsler wants to break it down for parts, but I just threaten to down tools and he backs off pretty quick." Then she became more contemplative again, "So, you're a courier runner? That's actually kinda anticlimactic..."

Hudson's eyebrows raised up, "There's nothing wrong with doing courier runs."

"I didn't say there was," replied Liberty, "it's just a bit ordinary and, well, you don't look like an ordinary guy to me."

Hudson stroked the bottom of his chin with his forefinger, contemplating how much to tell the curious young engineer. He wasn't sure why, but she engendered trust, and trust was a commodity that Hudson had run low on recently.

"I guess it depends on your definition of ordinary," said Hudson. Then he pointed up to the cockpit, "Mind if we take a look inside?"

Liberty smiled again and waved him on, before following him up the metal staircase to the open docking hatch. Hudson went directly to the cockpit – he could have found it with his eyes shut

– and dropped into the pilot's seat. Liberty arrived a few seconds later and slid into the second seat.

"If you really want the truth, until a few days ago I was an RGF cop," said Hudson, admiring the switchgear and the layout of the cockpit. It was a hundred times better designed than the stripped-down RGF Patrol Crafts. Then he looked over at Liberty, who had been strangely quiet. She was staring back at him as if he'd just spat on the deck.

"You're in the RGF?" she asked, but in a manner that sounded like she was enquiring whether Hudson was in league with the devil.

"I *was*..." Hudson said, emphasizing 'was'. "I quit, but then they fired me anyway, bankrupted me, and stranded me on Brahms Three."

Liberty's mouth fell open a little, "Why did you get fired?"

"I quit before they fired me..." Hudson reiterated; this was still a point of honor for him. Then he grabbed the control column of the VCX-110 and let out a slow breath, as the past again entered his thoughts. "It's a long story, Liberty. But the short version is that they represent everything I don't want to be. They take advantage of people, and sometimes they hurt people too."

"But you must have known they were corrupt, before signing up?" asked Liberty.

This had been a common question, which always came off sounding like an accusation to Hudson. Basically, they were saying, 'you should have known better.' It still riled him, but only because it was true. "A few people told me, but I didn't listen," Hudson replied.

Liberty again went back to studying Hudson as he continued to stroke the controls, lost in his own thoughts. She didn't press him further; instead, they both stared out of the cockpit glass across the bay. The sight of the calm ocean waves helped to soothe Hudson's battered soul.

"So, what is the reason you need a ship?" Liberty said, breaking the silence, though her voice lacked its earlier prickliness.

"I'm going to be a relic hunter," said Hudson, but then he snorted a derisory laugh. "Or that was the plan, anyway. But my measly one hundred and fifty thousand credits would barely pay for one of the engines in this ship."

"A relic hunter?" Liberty repeated back to him, her voice rising in pitch and volume. Then she became coyer, "But they're all crooks and mercenaries, like the RGF, aren't they? Not to be trusted?"

Hudson thought of the relic hunters he'd encountered, and it was true that many of them fit Liberty's description pretty well. But it wasn't true of them all. Ericka had been different, and so was Ma from the Landing Strip on Brahms Three. And though Tory Bellona was most definitely a mercenary, she certainly wasn't without honor.

"Not all of them," said Hudson, smiling over at Liberty, who had folded her legs up onto the seat. "The way I see it, each person chooses who they want to be. And I choose to find my scores without screwing others over." Liberty didn't respond, but she was still watching him carefully as Hudson continued to admire the ship. "Hell, it doesn't matter anyway. Unless I stumble across a briefcase full of hardbucks, I'm trapped on Earth, just like this beautiful ship here."

Liberty rocked the second seat from side to side. She had her oil-stained fingers pressed together in a cradle, and looked pensive. Hudson couldn't work out if she was just bored of him wasting her time, or reflecting on what he'd told her. Either way, sitting in the cockpit of the VCX-110 was beginning to make him feel depressed, knowing that he was probably a million credits short of ever owning it.

"I'm sorry, I've taken up enough of your time, already," he said, pushing himself out of the pilot's chair. "I'll let you get back to work."

Hudson's backside had barely left the padded seat when Liberty said, "She will fly."

"What's that?"

"This ship, she'll fly. I just make it seem like she's crippled so Swinsler can't sell her."

Hudson planted himself back down in the seat and rubbed the back of his head, "But why would you do that?"

"Like I said, I love this ship," replied Liberty, "so, the only person I'll let Swinsler sell it to is me. And since he thinks it's a write off, I know he'll let it go for a steal."

"How much?" asked Hudson, now hanging off Liberty's every word.

"Three hundred, maybe less."

Hudson nearly fell off the seat. "Three, for this? And you say you can make it fly?"

"I can," said Liberty, without even the slightest suggestion of doubt.

Hudson flopped back in the seat and shook his head. He then rested his hand on the lapel of Ericka's old leather jacket, feeling for the crystal. *Maybe selling this is the price I'll have to pay,* he wondered. It was certainly true that keeping the crystal was pointless if he couldn't reach any of the portal worlds. Scavenging inside the wrecks was the only way to hunt for its companion. Then he frowned, realizing something odd about Liberty's earlier admission.

"Why are you telling me about the ship?" he asked, squinting across at her. "Now I know it's not a carcass like the others, I could come back here and buy it."

Liberty smiled, "I don't think you'd do that, not after me telling you how much I love it."

Hudson considered slipping into his 'tough guy' relic hunter persona and arguing back, but he doubted Liberty would buy it.

"That's a pretty big assumption," Hudson replied. Liberty's statement had intrigued him. "Why do you think that, especially after me admitting I used to be a crooked RGF clobber?"

Liberty shrugged, "Just a feeling, I guess. I know ships and I know people, that's all."

Hudson looked around the cockpit and nodded, "Well, you certainly know your ships, I'll give you that. And I hope you're right about knowing people too. It makes a change to have someone not think I'm an idiot."

"I never said you weren't an idiot," replied Liberty, with a smirk. Hudson rolled his eyes, but then Liberty was quick to add, "Anyway, I have a proposition for you..."

This interested Hudson enough to let Liberty's snide comment slide. He pushed himself upright in the chair and turned to face her. "Oh? What proposition is that?"

"You put down your one fifty as a holding deposit on the VCX-110," Liberty began, to wide-eyed astonishment from Hudson, "and then you and I go relic hunting, bag a decent score, and buy this ship together."

CHAPTER 5

It took a few moments for Hudson's brain to fully register what Liberty had suggested, but he still felt the need to check that he'd heard her correctly. "Hang on, let me get this straight," he said, shuffling further forward on the seat. "You want me to put all my credits down as a deposit on this ship, and then go relic hunting with you?"

"Clearly, old age hasn't affected your hearing yet," replied Liberty. From the stark look on her face the snarky response wasn't intended to be humorous, and Hudson wasn't laughing. "Swinsler will break the VCX-110 apart and auction off the engines the moment I walk out of here. A deposit is the only way to make sure it stays safe. I have some money saved up; enough to buy the relic hunter licenses and two transport tickets to the closest portal world. After that, it's up to us."

"Do you have any idea what relic hunting actually involves?" asked Hudson. He was amazed at how casually she had made the suggestion. It was as if she had proposed nothing more complicated or unusual than popping to the local store to buy some groceries. "Have you even been off-world before?"

"No, I haven't been off-world before, but I don't see what that has to do with anything," said Liberty, with a flash of annoyance. "And yes, I do know what relic hunting involves."

"In theory, maybe," replied Hudson, aware that he was coming across a little condescending, but finding it hard to reign it in. Liberty's suggestion just seemed so fanciful. "But, there's a world of difference between theory and actually going on a hunt. The portal worlds are dangerous, and normal laws and rules don't apply inside those alien wrecks. This isn't a game, Liberty. People get hurt and even die on these hunts."

Liberty swung her legs off the seat and spun it to face him. She looked to be fighting hard to hold back her anger, but it was clear to Hudson that he'd pissed her off.

"You think you're the first person to tell me I can't do something?" Liberty began, holding Hudson's eyes with a vice-like grip. "I get it; you look at me and just see a girl with crazy ideas who has no clue how the world works."

"Hey, I didn't say that," Hudson hit back, though if he was honest, he had thought it.

"You didn't have to," replied Liberty, folding her arms to stop them from shaking. "I've been on my own since I was thirteen; on the streets, fighting to survive. I know how to take care of myself, and to handle myself, because I've had no choice." Liberty stopped to take a breath, but Hudson didn't interrupt; the fire in her belly had built up and she had to let it out. "But I've survived. For seven years I've survived and built a life here. But I want more." Then she looked around the cockpit, which seemed to have a soothing influence on her agitated mood. "I want to see the galaxy." Then she met Hudson's eyes again. "I don't just want to survive, I want to live."

Hudson felt a shiver run down his spine; it was like Liberty's words had caused an electric current to flow through his body. However, he was then suddenly back in the cargo hold of the light freighter above Brahms Three, holding Ericka's dead body in his arms. He shut his eyes and turned away.

"I hear you, Liberty, honestly, I really do," said Hudson, "and I don't doubt that you're a fighter. But there are people who want to hurt me, and if you're with me, they could hurt you too. I can't be responsible for that."

"I don't need a protector, Hudson, I need a partner," said Liberty. "We'd look out for each other. Equal risk, equal reward."

Hudson stood up and paced around the rear of the cockpit, while Liberty watched him eagerly. He couldn't believe he was contemplating it, but as crazy as her suggestion was, it might actually work. A ship the size of the VCX-110 would benefit from a second crewmember, and Liberty clearly had an aptitude for fixing things. Plus, he couldn't deny that the idea of someone having his back for a change was appealing. Then he kept thinking about Ericka, and how Griff and Cutler still had a score to settle with him. It wasn't fair to put that burden on Liberty too.

"Look, I can't deny that I'm tempted, but you don't want me as a partner," said Hudson. "I'm bad news. The last time I teamed up with someone, she ended up dead."

"I'll take that chance," replied Liberty, again without reservation.

Hudson did laugh this time. He'd laid it all on the table and the young woman hadn't batted an eyelid. "What the hell makes you so sure? I could be a serial killer for all you know."

"You don't look like a serial killer," replied Liberty, dismissively.

"Oh, well that settles it then," snorted Hudson.

"What? First, you're annoyed that I think you look like a music professor..."

"I thought it was art?" Hudson interrupted, layering on the sarcasm.

"Art, music, whatever..." Liberty replied, scowling at him, "But now you're annoyed because I *don't* think you look like a murderer?"

"Honestly, it's probably the nicest thing you've said about me so far, so I'll take it," said Hudson, smiling.

"Anyway, what makes you so sure that *I* won't strangle *you* in your sleep?" Liberty added. "You know as much about me as I know about you."

Hudson shrugged, "Intuition, I guess. I've known a lot of grade-A assholes over the years and have tuned my radar to detect them. You check out." Then he paused for effect and added, "So far..."

Liberty smiled, "Thanks for the vote of confidence." Then her expression hardened a touch. "Look, I realize this all seems crazy, but I have a feeling about you too. You're a pretty open book, Hudson Powell, and there's something about you that I don't see in a lot of people these days."

Hudson raised an eyebrow, "Gullibility?" he suggested, with a slight smirk.

"Decency," said Liberty, completely straight-faced.

Hudson sighed, "That's not always a trait that's served me well," he replied, realizing how doing the right thing had rarely worked in his favor. "But I appreciate it, thanks."

"So, do we have an agreement, Hudson Powell, ex RGF cop and wannabe relic hunter?"

"An agreement is usually fair," said Hudson, realizing that the terms of their barter were more than a little lopsided. "I put down a hundred and fifty grand up-front, but then we split the ship, fifty-fifty? I might be decent, but I'm no mug."

"Without me, this ship isn't going anywhere," Liberty replied, without hesitation. She'd clearly already prepared an answer to Hudson's question. "It would cost you double your deposit to get another shipyard to fix it up." Then she smiled, "Besides, you also get the pleasure of my company."

Hudson shook his head. He couldn't believe what he was about to do, but it was just the continuation of a succession of crazy events. And something Liberty had said still resonated with him. *I don't want to survive. I want to live.* Hudson had merely survived for the last twenty years. Now it was time to live.

"I must be out of my mind," said Hudson, extending a hand towards Liberty. "But, Liberty Devan, ace engineer and soon-to-be royal pain in my ass, we have a deal."

CHAPTER 6

Hudson toyed with his empty whiskey tumbler while he stared down at the two new relic hunter ID cards on the table. It had turned out to be far easier to acquire the licenses than he had imagined. It had merely involved the usual tedium of bureaucratic form-filling, followed by the handing over of a fat wedge of cash. The latter had been supplied to Hudson by Liberty Devan, without any reservations.

Remarkably, the young engineer had handed Hudson the money – a good chunk of her personal savings – before he'd even paid the deposit on the VCX-110. This spoke volumes about the amazing level of trust she had placed in him. Hudson didn't understand why he merited it. However, it made him feel good to know there was at least one person in the galaxy who believed in him.

Initially, the ease with which he'd acquired the licenses made him wonder why more people didn't sign up to be hunters. Then he'd got to the fine print of the license agreement and everything had become clear. It was full of fun little phrases, such as, 'By accepting this license you hereby waive all rights under CET, MP and OPW law while operating inside alien wreck sites.' Or, in other words, if you enter a wreck, you're on your own... He also enjoyed the entry, 'Should you be killed while operating inside an alien wreck, you hereby agree that the RGF can seize all assets up to the cost of any recovery operation to retrieve and repatriate your body, without limitation.' In RGF speak that basically meant they could take you for everything you had, just as they had done to Hudson, though under different circumstances.

For most people, the relic hunter license would have read like a permit to forfeit your life and your assets. Yet none of the legal jargon had deterred Hudson in the slightest. All it amounted to was a giant disclaimer that allowed the controlling authorities to wash their hands of the hunters, should they come to a sticky end. At the same time, it granted the RGF even more opportunities to rip people off – alive or dead. Hudson had seen enough of the CET and RGF in action to know that – license agreement or not – both organizations would act the same way, regardless. The license hunter agreement just created less paperwork.

Hudson knew what he was getting himself into, and was prepared to accept the risks. He'd already witnessed the chaos inside a wreck first hand, and right now he had nothing to lose. Then he looked down at Liberty's ID card, studying the young, serious face staring back at him. He hoped that she really was prepared for what awaited them. And he hoped she was genuinely as tough and wily as she'd claimed to be. Because making it out of the alien wreck with a decent score would require all of their combined guile and fortitude.

Hudson heard the door to the bar swing open, and looked up, expecting to see Liberty breeze in with the transport tickets. But instead of blue-grey coveralls, he saw the unmistakable blue-black uniform of the RGF. "Shit..." cursed Hudson, under his breath, as he recognized the two officers. The first was Corporal Violet Hodges and the second was her partner, Officer Ricky Yang. Both had been in the same unit as Hudson, and while neither was as abhorrent and detestable as Logan Griff, they both registered strongly on Hudson's asshole radar.

Hudson shuffled his chair to the side so that his back was to the bar, hoping that neither of the two would recognize him. Thankfully, the two RGF cops just proceeded to the counter without paying much attention to the rest of the room. Hudson let out a breathy sigh and then topped up his tumbler with another shot from the whiskey bottle he'd bought with Liberty's hardbucks. It was like drinking milk compared to the stuff Ma served up, but its warming and mildly soporific effect was still welcome.

The door opened again and Hudson glanced over, careful that no-one at the bar could see his face. He saw Liberty appear inside and stop just past the threshold. She peered around the room, until she spotted Hudson at the small table by the window, and then waved at him.

"Hudson! I got them!" she called out, as if she were talking about tickets to ringside seats at the next WrestleMania. Then she hurried over to him, drawing annoyed stares from other patrons of the bar, whose quiet afternoon drinks Liberty's hollering had just shattered.

Hudson tried to act as if Liberty's call wasn't aimed at him, and then chanced another quick glance towards the bar. This time Hodges and Yang were looking straight at him. He pressed his eyes shut and swore again, before turning away sharply and silently cursing his luck.

"Are you taking a nap?"

Hudson opened his eyes to see Liberty slide into the chair opposite, smiling broadly.

"We're going to need to work on you being a little more discreet," said Hudson, humorlessly. "Relic hunting is a sneaky business, which means not announcing who we are to a bar full of people."

"My, aren't we grumpy?" replied Liberty. Then she noticed the ID card on the table and picked it up excitedly.

"You look like a youth offender in that photo," said Hudson, grinning and taking another swig of whiskey.

Liberty scowled and then peered down at the photo on Hudson's license. "Hmm, I take it back, you actually *do* look like a serial killer."

Hudson quickly snatched back his license and slipped it into his jacket pocket. He then picked up the half-empty bottle of whiskey. "Speaking of killing," he said as he poured a measure into a clean tumbler on the table, filling it to the brim. "We need to seal our arrangement properly, through the act of murdering some brain cells."

Liberty looked at the glass and then turned up her nose, "Ugh, no way, that stuff tastes worse than mouthwash."

"As your captain, I insist," said Hudson, sliding the tumbler towards Liberty, spilling some of the contents onto the table as he did so.

"We're in this fifty-fifty, remember, so why do you get to be captain?"

Hudson sat back in the chair and held up his glass, "Can you fly a VCX-110?"

Liberty scowled again, "Well, no, not exactly..."

"Then that makes me the captain," said Hudson, smirking, "Now, have a drink with your captain or you'll hurt his feelings."

"Fine," growled Liberty, picking up the tumbler, "If it will shut you up."

They both knocked back the contents in one, but while Hudson swallowed the amber liquor as effortlessly as water, Liberty looked like she was experiencing a medical emergency.

"What is this crap?!" she coughed, spluttering spittle over her new ID card. "It tastes like hydraulic fluid..."

Hudson laughed and then re-filled his own tumbler, leaving Liberty's empty. "You get used to it. So, where are we headed?"

Liberty wiped the water from her eyes with the back of her hand and then reached through the slits in her coveralls. She pulled out a plastic wallet with the name, 'Yellow Line Trans-Portal Shuttles' written on it. She opened the wallet and handed Hudson one of two tickets inside. "The closest and cheapest portal world is Bach Two, so that's our next stop."

"Bach Two?" queried Hudson. He knew the planet pretty well, but there wasn't much call for extensive RGF patrols there anymore. As one of the first portal worlds (and alien wrecks) discovered, the hulk had been pretty much picked clean over the decades. Hudson knew the chances of finding a score that would cover the outstanding balance for the VCX-110 was pretty slim.

"Is there a problem with Bach Two?" asked Liberty, looking a little concerned.

Hudson considered a lie, but he didn't want to keep secrets from Liberty. And even a white lie was still a lie. Then he remembered about the alien crystal tucked inside the hidden compartment and realized he should tell her about that too. But a crowded bar with a couple of loitering RGF cops nearby wasn't the place to do it.

"Hudson? Is there a problem with Bach Two?" Liberty repeated, since Hudson hadn't answered.

"I was just thinking that finding a good score on the wreck there is going to be difficult," said Hudson, returning his attention to Liberty. The young engineer's head dropped, and a streak of blue hair fell across her face. Hudson didn't want to put a downer on what should have been a celebratory moment, and so quickly added, "But I'm up for the challenge; how about you?"

Liberty smiled, "Bring it on." Then she poured herself a shot from the whiskey bottle and downed it, before crumpling forward on the table in another coughing fit.

Hudson laughed, but then he spotted something about the ticket that wiped the smile from his face. "Hey, these tickets are one way!"

Liberty sat back up, thumping her chest with the palm of her hand. "Yeah, that's all I could afford with the hardbucks I had left."

"You do know that it rains for two hundred out of the three hundred days in the year on Bach Two?" said Hudson. If he'd been wearing glasses, he would be peering at her over the rim, like a suspicious teacher.

"We won't get stuck there," Liberty hit back, seeing where Hudson was leading.

"And in the summer, the scavenger town is plagued by tiny biting insects that swarm in groups so thick it looks like smoke..."

Liberty scowled, "We won't get stuck there..."

"And in the winter, it's dark for ninety per cent of the entire day..."

Liberty kicked him under the table, "Enough, already, I get it!" but she couldn't help laughing. "We won't get stuck there. Have a little faith, Hudson Powell."

"We're going to need a little more than faith, but what the hell," Hudson replied, slipping the ticket into his pocket and then raising his glass. "Let's take a one-way trip to one of the most annoying planets in the galaxy."

"That's the spirit," said Liberty, reaching for the whiskey bottle, but before she could pour the contents, a shadow crept across their table. They both looked up to see two RGF cops looking down at them, thumbs tucked into their belts. Liberty glanced across to Hudson, who was now rubbing his temple and trying to hide his face at the same time, before turning back to the two officers. "Is there a problem?"

"The problem is I don't like drinking in bars that let stinking traitors inside," said the woman.

Liberty was about to answer, when Hudson cut in. "Violet, what a pleasure it is to see you again. Your face looks positively radiant." He then looked up at the officer and frowned, "Oh, sorry, that's just the sunburn." Liberty smirked, but the woman was not amused.

"That's Corporal Hodges to you, traitor," she replied, while subconsciously touching her face, as if testing its temperature. "Now, I think you should leave, before things get ugly."

Hudson drew in a deep breath and let it out. He didn't want a confrontation, but his tolerance for taking crap from the RGF had run out long ago. He pushed his chair back across the tiled floor, causing it to screech like someone drawing their fingernails across a blackboard. Then he stood up and faced off against Hodges.

"I can call you whatever the hell I like, Violet," said Hudson, glowering at the stern older woman. "And I can drink wherever I like too. If you have a problem with that then you can shove it up your uptight, saggy ass."

Hodges smiled; she loved conflict and seemed pleased that Hudson had bitten back, rather than turned tail. She glanced over to Liberty, looking her up and down with distain. "Who is that?" she said, meeting Hudson's eyes again. "Got yourself a new girlfriend already?" Then her lips curled into a cruel smile, "It was such a shame what happened to the last one..."

Hudson snapped and blinded by rage he shoved Hodges hard on the chest, sending her crashing backward into another table. He was ready to advance, when Yang drew his weapon and leveled it at him.

"Get back, now!" Yang yelled, as Hodges pulled herself off the table. Suddenly a dozen more chairs screeched across the tiled floor, as other patrons quickly scampered away. It was like the scene of a Wild West tavern shootout, except no-one had started shooting – at least not yet. Unseen by Hudson, Liberty had also stood up and moved off to the side of Yang, but she remained silent.

Hodges strode back up to Hudson, teeth gritted and body clenched tighter than her fists. "You're going to regret that, traitor," she snarled, words seething through the gaps in her toothy grimace.

Hudson had recovered some of his composure, but he was still in no mood for being pushed around. "This isn't a portal world; you don't have any authority here." Then he looked at Yang, who still had the weapon on him. "And we both know you won't shoot me. So just get the hell out of my way."

Hodges slammed a kick into Hudson's gut, sucker punching him while his attention was distracted. The blow stole Hudson's breath away, and forced him to double over in pain. "Oh, I'm not done with you yet, traitor," said Hodges, grabbing a thick tuft of Hudson's hair and yanking his head back. "Me and Yang here are going to have some fun first. Isn't that right, Officer Yang?"

Yang didn't have a chance to answer, because Liberty had darted towards him, grabbed his wrists and stripped the weapon from his hand. Hudson looked on as she then struck Yang with a forearm, sending the officer staggering back.

Hudson shook off Hodges, but he was still too winded to fight. "Run!" he barked, struggling to achieve any volume. "Liberty, run, get out!"

Yang recovered and together with Hodges they both rounded on Liberty. Both officers drew riot batons.

"That was a big mistake, girl..." growled Yang, teasing the end of the baton towards Liberty.

Hudson staggered forwards, trying to intervene, but as Hodges raised her weapon, ready to strike, he was powerless to help.

Hudson watched as the baton swung towards Liberty, however instead of being struck, she deflected the attack, before spinning on the heels of her heavy safety boots and snapping a fast kick into Yang's chest. The officer was taken completely by surprise and staggered backwards, an oily boot mark pressed onto his shirt. Hodges struck out again, but Liberty evaded, then blocked, and stripped the baton from her grasp, claiming it as her own. Hodges stood back, stunned by the ineffectiveness of her attacks and the fact she had been so easily disarmed. However, Liberty gave her no opportunity to attack again, hammering defensive strikes into the Corporal's shoulders and thighs. Hodges' legs gave way and she fell, grasping at her crushed muscles. Yang darted forward again, slashing his baton at Liberty's head. She blocked the attack and then turned into Yang, gripping his belt and sliding an arm underneath his for leverage. Before Yang knew what was happening, Liberty had thrown him down onto their table, collapsing it under the weight of the impact. Yang groaned, holding the back of his head, but he didn't try to stand.

Liberty picked up her transport ticket, which had scattered to the tiled floor after the table gave way, and went to help Hudson to his feet.

"I thought you were an engineer, not a damn ninja," said Hudson, holding his ribs.

"You're welcome," said Liberty, "but I think it's about time we left."

"No shit," said Hudson as they both swiftly headed for the door, passing other drinkers who were still hiding under tables. "Bach Two is sounding pretty appealing right now."

Liberty smiled, "What was that you said about me needing to be more discreet?"

There was a pause as Hudson looked into Liberty's eyes, before they both burst out laughing.

CHAPTER 7

The last trans-portal flight that Hudson had taken had been from Brahms Three to Earth, in order to fulfil Ericka Reach's dying wish. At that time, he was on the run from Logan Griff, broke, plagued with guilt, and clueless about how to rebuild the tattered remains of his life. Now, he was a licensed relic hunter, about to go on his first hunt. And he wasn't alone; he had a partner that he'd only just met, but felt like he'd known for years. The prize, should they manage to scavenge deep enough inside the wreck to bag a decent score, was a VCX-110 light courier runner. This was more than just a ship, Hudson thought to himself – it was freedom.

What a difference two weeks can make, he mused, while looking out of the small porthole window. The transport had just begun its descent through the atmosphere of Bach Two, on course for the scavenger town.

"Come on, let's go to the front observation deck," said a giddy Liberty Devan, leaning across him to peer through the porthole. She then unbuckled her harness and sprang up as if it had been an ejector seat. "We'll get a better view of the wreck site."

Hudson felt like reminding her that he'd already flown into dozens of scavenger towns, and seen just as many wreck sites, but Liberty's enthusiasm was infectious.

"Come on!" she called out, already several rows ahead of him.

"Okay, already!" Hudson hollered back, "You go ahead; I'll catch you up."

Liberty didn't need telling twice. She had already climbed the spiral staircase to the observation level, before Hudson had even got out of his seat. As he wandered down the aisle, he caught sight of the spaceport arrivals board on one of the public infopanels. Something compelled him to read it, and he stopped to scan through the ship registries. As one of the more developed inner portal worlds, a couple of million people lived on Bach Two, spread out across several small cities. The scavenger town was one of them, and It was about ten times the size of the shipping-container town of Brahms Three. It was a bustling travel hub, though more for business travelers than for relic hunters. The majority of scavengers had moved on to more distant wrecks, where the risk levels and reward opportunities were both significantly higher.

He was about to carry on past the infopanel when one of the line entries caught his attention. It read, 'Landed: 09:52 Earth Standard | FS-31 Patrol Craft, Hawk-1333F'. He took a step closer to the panel, and peered at the entry. *Where have I seen that before?* he asked himself, feeling suddenly more anxious. The name had triggered something in his subconscious mind, but he couldn't dredge it back to the surface. Then Liberty ducked her head beneath the floor of the upper level and yelled at him again. *Hawk-1333F...* Hudson repeated in his mind, wracking his brains, but drawing a blank. Another holler from Liberty drew irritated glances from other passengers, which strangely were all directed at Hudson, rather than the woman doing the shouting. He left the infopanel and jogged up to Liberty, muttering apologies and platitudes to the passengers who scowled at him along the way.

"Look at that thing!" said Liberty, who was already standing by the window.

Hudson squeezed in amongst the other passengers who were also excitedly looking out at the wreck site. The transport was making its customary slow bank around the checkpoint perimeter to give its passengers a bird's eye view of the alien spectacle. The crashed hulk was half buried underneath Bach Two's muddy surface, but it was still an imposing sight. Hudson may have seen it and wrecks like it many times before, but despite his earlier indifference, he admitted to still being in awe of the giant alien ship.

"It's something else, right?" he said, "Wait till you see inside."

"You've already been on a hunt?" asked Liberty, looking up at him with her curious, azure eyes.

"No, not on a hunt, but I have been inside a wreck. Recently, in fact," replied Hudson, remembering the adventure that had led to his first meeting with Tory Bellona. "We need to be careful, though; other hunters set booby traps inside to catch out newbie scavengers like us."

"Figures," Liberty tutted. "But don't worry, I'm used to watching my step."

The transport veered away from the wreck and descended into the spaceport on the outskirts of the scavenger town. The change in scenery from spectacular to mundane caused most of the other onlookers to filter away. However, despite the frequent calls over the transport's PA system asking passengers to return to their seat, Hudson and Liberty remained in the observation lounge.

"Come on, we need to buy some gear, before starting our hunt," said Hudson, stumbling as the shuttle's landing struts touched down on the deck.

However, Liberty was still pressed to the window. "Hey, come on, there's nothing to see now."

"Speak for yourself," said Liberty, "this spaceport is like a supercar showroom for sexy spaceships."

Hudson smiled and returned to the window. Liberty wasn't wrong – besides the commercial shuttles and freighters, there was a wide diversity of privately-owned starships on stand too.

"Hey, avert your eyes, lady," said Hudson, waggishly. "We already have a ship. So long as we can find a score here to pay for it."

"Don't worry, I'm just window shopping; nothing here tops our VCX-110." Then she made a cooing noise and pointed across the deck. "Though that FS-31 is pretty badass too."

Hudson looked over to where Liberty was pointing and saw the ship in question. It was sleek and had an iridescent blue-black skin like a Grackle. Liberty was right, it was a handsome ship. Then he remembered it was the same model as the one that had caught his attention on the infopanel. *FS-31 Patrol Craft, Hawk-1333F*, Hudson remembered. Suddenly he felt his skin crawl and his stomach tighten in a knot. "Hawk-1333F..." he said out loud. "That ship is registry Hawk-1333F."

"So what?" asked Liberty.

"That's Cutler Wendell's ship," replied Hudson, staring out at the shimmering vessel. "That's the ship owned by the asshole who's trying to kill me."

CHAPTER 8

The equipment stores in the larger scavenger towns were like toy shops to a fully-grown man like Hudson Powell. While there were usually several to choose from, apart from on the more distant portal worlds, the leading supplier was a chain called 'Scavenger's Paradise'. Hudson could never contain his smiles as he walked through the large revolving doors, which were a trademark feature of the brand. He was standing just inside the foyer of the Scavenger's Paradise on Bach Two, grinning like a proverbial Cheshire cat. It was a welcome distraction that had temporarily stopped him fretting about whether Cutler was about to knife him in the back. As he glanced across at Liberty he was pleased to note that her expression was a mirror of his own.

"You shouldn't have brought me in here," said Liberty, her eyes popping out as if on stalks. "I'm going to buy the entire store..."

"I'm afraid we don't have quite enough hardbucks left to do that," said Hudson, acting as Liberty's inner voice of reason. "We'll have to restrict ourselves to essential provisions."

"Spoilsport," replied Liberty, with a slightly petulant huffiness. "What essential provisions do we need, anyway?"

Hudson rubbed his stubbled chin; he hadn't managed to shave since departing Earth. "You know what; I have no idea." Then he looked at Liberty's vintage Royal Air Force coveralls, which were already a little worse for wear. "I'd suggest you sort yourself out with some more appropriate clothing, though."

"More appropriate?" Liberty repeated, clearly taking offense at the suggestion that there was something wrong with her attire. She caressed the fabric of her coveralls, lovingly. "This is a classic. And very practical."

"For working on starship engines, maybe," said Hudson, "but for relic hunting, you need something hard wearing, and with plenty of pockets."

"Fair point, I suppose I can check out what they have," replied Liberty, reluctantly agreeing with Hudson. "But I'm still keeping these coveralls."

"I had no doubt you would," said Hudson, then he grinned mischievously and sniffed the air. "Perhaps give them a wash first, though..."

Liberty slapped him on the arm, but she was smiling too. Then she took the lead, heading off down the nearest aisle. "Come on, let's browse a little. I'm sure inspiration will strike."

"Remember, we're looking for essentials," reiterated Hudson, concerned about what might constitute as 'essential' in the mind of Liberty Devan. "Things we might need to get around inside a pitch-black alien wreck that wasn't designed for humans."

"I'm on it, skipper," said Liberty, saluting lazily as she raced off down one of the many aisles. "I'll start with rucksacks, water bottles, and some lights. You look for climbing gear, or something along those lines. If what you said about this wreck is true, we might need to venture into some harder to reach areas."

Hudson watched Liberty hurry off, and again felt himself being boosted by her infectious enthusiasm. She was also right about the need to discover somewhere inside the hulk that few other hunters had already found. Otherwise, they'd end up with a score that was barely able to buy them return tickets to Earth.

Hudson grabbed a small trolley and began to wander along the aisles. However, given the size and maze-like layout of the store, it was still several minutes before he found one that contained climbing equipment. He browsed along the shelves, not really knowing what he was looking for, and found a pack of suction clamps. Hudson recalled how the walls of the strange, hexagonal corridors inside the alien wrecks had smooth, metallic surfaces. The suction clamps would be a good choice for attaching ropes to, he reckoned, and threw them into his trolley.

"Buy them if you want to die..."

Hudson spun around and saw Tory Bellona leaning against the opposite rack of shelves. Despite the fact she was likely here to kill him, he smiled, realizing that he was glad to see her.

"Thanks for the tip," said Hudson, placing the suction clamps back on the shelf.

Tory walked up in front of Hudson and then reached up to a shelf behind his head, before pulling down a bag of climbing pitons. She was so close that Hudson could smell the fragrance of the shampoo she'd used on her hair. He caught a hint of coconut and vanilla, which only made Tory seem more exotic and exciting than he already thought she was.

Tory threw the bag into Hudson's trolley and then stepped back. "Use these instead. They will penetrate through the walls and clamp on from behind. The suction cups always fall off, taking the hunters with them."

Hudson smiled, "Forgive me for being a little suspicious of your motives," he said, "since I'm guessing you're here to kill me."

"I can't claim the bounty if you fall to your death first," replied Tory. The response was so deadpan that Hudson couldn't tell if she was joking or not.

"How did you know I was here?"

Tory strolled a little further up the aisle, tossing a number of other items into Hudson's trolley as she went. "We heard about your little altercation with the RGF in San Francisco," she said, occasionally glancing back at Hudson. "For a man with a target on his back, you should be keeping more of a low profile."

"I'm not going to spend my life hiding from scumbags like Cutler and Griff," said Hudson. "I assume he's not here with you at the moment? Cutler, I mean."

"I know who you mean," said Tory, "and no, he's not in the store, but he will be inside the wreck, looking for you. And so will I."

"I'll keep that in mind," replied Hudson. The tone of the conversation had become hostile, like two boxers at a pre-match press conference. Despite this, Tory had continued to fill Hudson's trolley with items from the shelves as they wandered along the aisle together.

Tory then stopped and looked Hudson over from top to toe, as if she were an army drill sergeant, inspecting him on parade. "You're not armed," she said, meeting his eyes again.

"Funds are a bit tight," admitted Hudson. Then he pointed to the contents of the trolley and added, "I may not even have enough to pay for this little lot."

Tory shook her head, then removed her armor-reinforced jacket. Underneath she wore a tight, black tank top. Hudson caught himself checking her out, before forcing himself to look away. *Get a grip, Hudson, she's trying to kill you, not seduce you...* he told himself. Though it was becoming more difficult to know which was actually the case. In addition to the tank top she also wore a shoulder holster with a compact sidearm tucked inside. Compared to the huge single-action revolver on her belt, the weapon looked a bit puny. She removed the holster and handed it to Hudson.

"Here, take this," said Tory. "Trust me, you're going to need it."

Hudson took the weapon, which was warm from Tory's body heat, but then shook his head, "I can't pay you for this."

"Then make sure you stay alive long enough to give it back," said Tory, pulling her jacket back on.

Hudson nodded and then removed his own leather jacket, handing it to Tory to hold while he put on the holster. At the same time, Liberty rounded the corner and started heading down the aisle towards them. She had taken Hudson's advice and ditched the coveralls for a slim-fitting black jacket and pants combination. It certainly met Hudson's requirement of being rugged and having plenty of pockets. As she got closer, she realized that Hudson wasn't alone and approached more cautiously.

Tory squeezed the tough leather jacket between her fingers, her eyes narrowing. "Do you still have it?" she asked, as Liberty stopped a few paces away, drawing inquisitive glances from Tory. Then she added, vaguely, "The object..."

"I still have it," said Hudson, while offering a reassuring smile to Liberty. He then extended a hand and waited for Tory to hand back the jacket. Tory hesitated, clearly fighting her more mercenary instincts to simply take what she wanted, before shoving the jacket into Hudson's hand.

"You should have sold it while you had the chance," said Tory. "Or before someone like me takes it from you." Then she glanced across to Liberty and the two women exchanged icy stares. "Who is this?"

The question was aimed at Hudson, but Liberty didn't give him a chance to answer. "This is his partner, Liberty Devan," she said, holding Tory's eyes without blinking. "And who the hell are you?"

Tory smiled, "Someone you don't want to mess with, Liberty Devan," she said, with an incongruously affable tone. "Then she looked back at Hudson and pressed a hand to his side, where the pistol was now concealed. Her sudden touch made Hudson flinch, but it also gave him a thrill. He felt like a teenager again. "If you see me in the wreck, make sure you're ready to use that," Tory said, with feeling. "Because you can be sure that other hunters will shoot first, and not bother asking any questions later." Then she glanced back at Liberty again, holding her eyes for a second longer than seemed natural, before turning on her heels, and walking away.

Hudson let out a low whistle. He didn't know whether he was shit-scared or aroused, or both. "Well, that was fun," he said, turning to Liberty, who unceremoniously dumped the gear she was carrying into the trolley.

"Care to tell me who that was, and why she was giving you a weapon?" Liberty looked distinctly pissed off.

"I'll fill you in on the way to the checkpoint district," said Hudson, realizing that he owed her an explanation. Then he remembered about the crystal, and ushered Liberty back along the aisle until they reached a changing room. He beckoned Liberty inside and then pulled the curtain back.

"What are you doing? I don't want to try anything else on," said Liberty, "and I sure as hell wouldn't do it with you gawping at me."

"Just quit your yammering for a second, will you?" snapped Hudson, reaching into the compartment in his jacket. Liberty looked about ready to pop him on the nose, but then she saw the crystal and her mouth fell open slightly.

"What is that?" she said, as Hudson handed the relic to her.

"No-one knows," said Hudson. "It came from the alien wreck on Brahms Three."

"How did you get it?" said Liberty, turning the crystal over in her hands, as delicately as if it were a priceless Ming Dynasty vase.

"That's part of what I need to fill you in on," replied Hudson. "An assessor on Earth suggested it could be some kind of transceiver. He reckoned it may have been missing a piece. If we can find something to match, this thing could be worth a fortune."

"It already is," said Liberty, offering the relic back to Hudson. "This could have paid for the VCX-110 and then some. Why haven't you sold it already?"

Hudson took the crystal and concealed it back inside his jacket. "Because this is why we're out here, Liberty. Think about it – we have the chance to discover something no-one has ever found before. The chance to become famous. Doesn't that sound like living to you?"

Liberty cocked her head to the side and pouted, "It won't do us any good if your girlfriend out there takes it from your cold, dead body."

Hudson scowled, "If she'd wanted to, she could have taken it from me already." Then he sighed, trying to figure out how best to explain their association, before realizing he had no idea how to categorize it himself. "Let's just say that Tory Bellona and I have a... complicated relationship."

"Does that relationship involve her trying to kill us both inside the alien wreck?" asked Liberty, folding her arms.

Hudson chewed the inside of his mouth for a moment and then smiled. "I told you this would be a challenge, didn't I?..."

CHAPTER 9

Hudson handed his relic hunter ID card to the RGF officer stationed at the entrance gate to the checkpoint district. Thankfully, this was an officer he'd never seen before, but Hudson still waited nervously as the man scanned the card. It was possible Griff or Wash had put him on some sort of special watch list. After an agonizing few seconds the officer lazily handed back the ID and ushered Hudson through the Shaak radiation detector. Purple beams of light scanned Hudson's entire body as he passed between the detector's two pillars. Then the display flashed up, 'Shaak Radiation: Negative', and Hudson breathed a sigh of relief. The shielded internal compartment inside his jacket was still doing an effective job of concealing the crystal.

Liberty followed immediately after, but as she reached Hudson's side, she appeared to be in a daze, staring up at the towering outer hull of the alien wreck.

"And you thought it looked big on the approach to the spaceport...", said Hudson, envious of how Liberty must have been feeling at that moment. He'd never forgotten the sheer exhilaration he'd experienced the very first time he had been this close to an alien wreck.

"I've read about these ships all my life," said Liberty, as awestruck as if she were peering up at a rock star idol. "It blows my mind to think about where they came from and who built them. And also why they ended up broken and scattered across so many worlds." Then she looked up at Hudson, eyes still burning with wonder, "Do you think about it too?"

"Of course," Hudson replied, smiling. "It's the single greatest mystery of all time." Then he patted his jacket. "Maybe this little crystal could help unlock it."

Liberty nodded and went back to staring up at the ship, "You were right not to sell it. It's too important."

Hudson looked at Liberty and recognized the hunger in her eyes. He could practically feel the electricity pulsing through her body. "How do you feel, Liberty?" he asked her, already knowing what her answer would be, because he instinctively knew he felt the same.

"Alive…" said Liberty, glancing up at Hudson and smiling. "I feel alive."

"Then let's go relic hunting," declared Hudson, taking his pack off his back and setting it down. "But first, we need to know where the hell we're going."

"First we need to actually get inside," Liberty corrected him.

"That's the easy part," said Hudson, while removing a folded sheet of epaper from his rucksack. He opened it to reveal a map of the hulk.

"Where did you get that?" asked Liberty, moving closer so she could study the intricate 3D model.

"Another donation from our friend Tory," said Hudson. "I found It In the trolley after she left the Scavenger's Paradise."

"*Your* friend…" Liberty corrected him, acidly. "For someone who is supposedly out to kill you, she's sure trying hard to keep you alive."

"I'm not complaining, and neither should you," replied Hudson. However, before Liberty could retort, he quickly turned back to the map. "It's the most accurate schematic of the alien hulks that there is. It's a composite of data gathered from dozens of scavenger expeditions, spanning decades."

Liberty scanned her eyes across the map, which was a complex maze of interconnected corridors and anonymous-looking hexagonal spaces of widely varying sizes. "This isn't like any ship layout

I've ever seen," she said rubbing her temples, "but then it is an order of magnitude larger than any ship us mere humans have built. Are you sure this helps us find the best place to hunt?"

"There's no 'X marks the spot' if that's what you're asking," said Hudson. There was a little more snark to his response than he'd intended, and he caught a dirty look in return. Then he quickly zoomed in on a section close to the center axis. "But I think here could be worth a look. From the descriptions of what was found there in the past, it sounds like it might be a control hub for the ship's navigational system. Or maybe a communication hub."

Liberty nodded, understanding Hudson's train of thinking, "A solid place to go searching for a crystal."

"Exactly..." said Hudson, folding up the map. He then pushed it into his jacket pocket and slung his rucksack back on. "There's an entry point in the mid-axis just over there. It's not far above ground level and there's already a scaffold in place to help hunters get in."

"Then let's go," said Liberty, with renewed zeal. However, she had barely taken a step forward, before Hudson saw Cutler Wendell and Tory Bellona heading their way.

"Hold up, Liberty," he called out, "we have a rodent problem to deal with first."

Liberty frowned back at him, before she too spotted the approaching pair.

"I want to thank you for making it so easy to find you again, Hudson Powell," said Cutler in his sinister, monotone drawl. Tory hung back a little at his side, thumbs pressed into her belt. The hem of her jacket was tucked behind the grip of her single-action revolver. She looked at Hudson, but didn't say anything. "Most people who dodged a bullet like you did would be smart enough to stay out of the line of fire. Now I'm really going to enjoy putting you down."

"I must have clobbered you over the head harder than I thought," said Hudson, slipping into his tough-guy relic hunter persona, "because that sounds like crazy talk..."

Cutler's lips curled into what would have been a smile on the face of any normal person. However, on Cutler it took on a somehow much darker edge. "We'll see..." he replied, with a snake-like hiss. "I'll see you inside." Then he turned to Liberty, offering a pretend doff of his non-existent cap, before walking off towards the wreck. Tory met Hudson's eyes for a second longer and then followed on behind Cutler.

"Wow, that guy is a real piece of work," said Liberty. "They make a great couple."

"She's not with him," Hudson was quick to add. Then he silently cursed himself, realizing he'd jumped to Tory's defense too quickly.

Liberty's eyes rolled back, "Oh no, don't tell me you're sweet on psycho lady?"

"Come on, we're wasting time," said Hudson, rushing ahead of Liberty to avoid answering the question.

Liberty shook her head, and followed on, "Just remember what we came here for," she shouted after him, "which, in case you've forgotten, is *not* Tory Bellona..."

CHAPTER 10

The checkpoint district was relatively quiet compared to the bustling scavenger town. Beyond perhaps a dozen hunter crews, most of the other people milling around were closely-monitored tourist parties or academic research groups. Hudson guessed there were perhaps at most another ten hunter crews already inside the wreck. As a result, given the scale of the vessel, Hudson figured they could largely avoid contact with potential rivals. That was, of course, apart from anyone that was specifically looking for them, such as Cutler Wendell.

Cutler had waited for Hudson and Liberty to enter the wreck first. He had casually waved them off, as if they were departing from a polite Friday night dinner party. But Hudson guessed that Cutler wouldn't follow straight away. He'd want to let them get deeper inside the ship first, so that any potential acts of murder went unnoticed. The usual laws may not have applied inside the alien vessels, but the RGF still had some authority. And they were keen to levy charges for damages to any hunter that became trigger-happy while inside.

Hudson and Liberty passed through the fracture in the hull using the scaffold that was already in place, and moved into the ship's interior. In front of them a corridor stretched out as far as Hudson could see, illuminated by a long strip of intense LED lights.

"Nice of them to add lights for us," said Liberty, moving ahead of Hudson, and running her hand across the alien metal of the wall.

"Most of the outer sections will have some form of lighting, either added by the RGF or left over from other hunters," said Hudson, looking at the map to get his bearings. "But the deeper we go, the darker and more dangerous it will get. So, stay on your toes... Especially because Cutler will be coming after us."

"Cutler *and* Tory," Liberty corrected him, but then cheerfully added, "But, you got it skipper." Being inside the alien wreck had put Liberty in an almost euphoric mood.

Hudson folded the map and shoved it back into his pocket, before glancing anxiously behind. He half-expected Cutler to already be there, weapon in hand. "Let's move; and move quickly. We need to put some distance between us and Cutler," said

Hudson, seeing a phantom of Cutler Wendell in every flickering shadow.

"Cutler *and* Tory..." Liberty corrected again, this time putting greater emphasis on 'and'. "She may be soft on you, but that won't stop her from using that archaic pistol on me, given half a chance."

"Fine, Cutler *and* Tory," Hudson replied, mimicking Liberty's stressing of 'and', before pointing towards where the corridors split off ahead of them. "We need to drop four levels, but carry on in this direction, at least for now. That should lead us into a larger open space. Then we check the map again and go from there."

Hudson and Liberty moved off along the corridor, taking advantage of ropes and ladders that were already in place. However, after falling foul of a greased rope in the wreck on Brahms Three, Hudson tested each one first in case of booby traps. After twenty minutes they reached the end of the fourth steeply-descending corridor, bringing them onto the target level Hudson was aiming for. They both then dropped down into a shallow, hexagonal space with the approximate area of an aircraft hangar. An array of metal beams jutted out from each surface, some of which disappeared through the floor or ceiling. Others appeared to crisscross towards a spherical object in the center, which was about the size of an observatory dome.

"Wow, what is this place?" wondered Liberty, admiring the unique architecture of the space.

"I have no idea," replied Hudson, grabbing the map again and sitting on his haunches. "At the RGF academy, they suggested that about eighty percent of these alien hulks were given over to power generation or distribution, and engines. The entire rear third of the ship is basically one giant propulsion system."

Liberty went ahead while Hudson studied the map, muttering to himself while trying to make sense of the maze of corridors. The central sphere looked to be made from an almost glassy material, except that it wasn't translucent. "This doesn't look like any power system I've ever seen," said Liberty. "It does sort of remind me of something, though."

Hudson joined Liberty and then ran his hand along the smooth alien metal. He couldn't detect any seams, as if the entire massive apparatus had been fabricated as a single piece.

Then Liberty clicked her fingers, "It's like a neuron!" she exclaimed, turning to Hudson. "Imagine the central sphere as a nucleus with the metal beams as Axons," she went on, as Hudson raised a puzzled eyebrow. "Perhaps this connects to other parts of the ship like synapses would do in a brain?"

"I hope you're wrong," said Hudson, uneasily. He stepped away from the sphere and returned to studying the map.

Liberty frowned, "Why do you say that?"

"Because if this thing has neurons and synapses and whatever that other thing was you said, maybe it used to think for itself," replied Hudson, squinting at the epaper. "A thinking ship sounds pretty creepy, if you ask me."

"Well, I think it sounds exciting," Liberty countered, now placing her hand on the metal sphere. "Think about it; we don't know even half of what the alien CPU tech is capable of. We've barely scratched the surface of its capabilities, so who knows what an advanced alien race could have already achieved."

Hudson had stopped listening. He'd seen a flicker at the far end of the room, close to where they had emerged into the hexagonal space. He took a few paces towards it, squinting in the low light.

"What is it?" said Liberty, stepping to his side. Hudson could hear the tension in her voice.

Suddenly two figures rushed out of cover and hid behind one of the crisscrossed metal beams. Despite the gloomy illumination, Hudson saw the flash of metal in their hands.

"Hudson, look out!" Liberty cried, as a shot rang out and a bullet pinged off the metal deck a few meters to their side.

Hudson and Liberty dashed towards another of the metal beams to take cover, but in his haste, Hudson accidently dropped the map.

"Damn it, Tory, you missed him!" came the voice of Cutler Wendell.

Hudson watched as Cutler darted out from behind cover and took up position behind another beam. Tory followed close behind him.

"I'm glad your mercenary friend's aim is as bad as her attitude," said Liberty, as they both hid behind the beam.

"Somehow, I don't think she missed by accident," replied Hudson. Then he spotted an opening on the wall closest to them. He nodded over to it, "Let's use these beams as cover and try to get to that corridor."

Liberty nodded and moved out ahead of Hudson, while both tried to keep half an eye on where Cutler was. However, the mercenary had vanished just as swiftly as he had appeared.

Hudson followed Liberty, ducking under one beam and then the next. The corridor entrance was getting closer, and Liberty pushed on towards it, growing less cautious with each new step. Suddenly Cutler sprang out from the shadows directly ahead. It was as if he'd literally appeared out of nowhere. Liberty froze as the mercenary raised his weapon.

"Liberty, move!" Hudson called out. He made a dash for her, but he was too late; Cutler squeezed the trigger and fired. Hudson flinched as the crack split the air, and then Liberty jolted, as if hit with an electric shock. But as Hudson looked on, panic gripping his body and mind, he glanced back towards Cutler and saw Tory's hand on Cutler's arm, steering his aim off to the side.

"We're not here for the girl," Tory snapped, as Cutler glowered at her, clearly furious at her intervention. "It's just heat we don't need. Focus on the traitor; he's our payday."

Cutler angrily yanked his arm away from Tory, as Liberty finally came to her senses and ran behind the central sphere. "What's gotten into you, Tory?" Cutler growled. "It makes no damn difference if she lives or dies; not in here."

Tory clicked back the hammer on her revolver, "You're forgetting why we're here," she hit back, with equal bite. "Just get the ex-cop; I'll make sure the girl stays quiet."

Cutler's eyes narrowed, "Make sure you do," he snarled, "I can't have you going soft." Then he moved off, circling around to where he'd seen Hudson run and hide.

Hudson kept a close watch on Cutler, but then saw Liberty peek out from behind the sphere. Tory was moving towards her, revolver held ready, hammer cocked. He was aware that Tory had pulled her punches twice already during their brief encounter, and he couldn't bank on her doing it for a third time.

Reaching inside his jacket, Hudson removed the pistol that Tory had given him and clicked off the safety. He chanced a look around the pillar to check on Cutler's whereabouts, when a sharp metallic chime rang out inches from his head. He ducked into cover again, and chastised himself for being so careless. Cutler wasn't just a common thief; he was a skilled bounty hunter. Hudson knew he was lucky to still be alive.

"Come out, come out, Hudson Powell," droned Cutler Wendell, "Just make it easy on yourself."

Hudson edged further along the pillar and tried to see where Liberty and Tory had gone, but his view of them was hindered by the sphere. "Shit..." Hudson cursed under his breath, as another round ricocheted off the metal.

"You can't escape," Cutler went on, as he continued to stalk Hudson, "I'll make you a deal; give yourself up now, and I'll let the girl live."

Hudson caught a glimpse of Cutler ducking under a nearby beam, creeping ever closer, and he fell back. Across the other side of the room, he could now make out Tory, carefully stepping to the side, one foot over the other, edging closer and closer to the sphere. Then he saw Liberty dart from cover and kick the weapon from Tory's hand, displaying the same agility she'd demonstrated in the bar brawl in San Francisco. Tory was stunned at first, but as Liberty pressed her attack, landing another kick to Tory's stomach, sending her reeling backwards, he could see the shape of her expression shift. He'd seen the look before, in the wreck on Brahms Three, before Hudson had helped save Tory from another crew of hunters. It was raw, animalistic and cruel. The gloves had just come off.

Two more rounds pinged off the metal beam Hudson was pressed up behind, snapping his attention back to his own perilous circumstances. Pain stung his thigh and he reached down, feeling blood wet his hand. He hadn't been shot; only nicked as the bullet raced past, but it had still been a lucky escape. He edged further into cover and grasped the pistol tightly, while forcing his breathing into a more regular rhythm. He was going to have to move fast, not only to save himself, but to help Liberty too. The young engineer could clearly handle herself in a fight. Maybe she was even a match for Tory Bellona in a hand-to-hand contest. However, Liberty was no match for a bullet from a powerful .44-40 caliber revolver.

"I'll make you a better deal, Cutler," Hudson shouted into the gloom. "Crawl back to that coward, Griff, and tell him to face me himself, and I'll let you walk out of here."

An insipid laugh reverberated around the room, "How are you going to do that, Mr. Powell?" Cutler called out, walking clearly into Hudson's line of sight. "I hacked your manifest after you cleared the border checkpoint; you don't even have any weapons."

Hudson laughed quietly to himself. The reason for Cutler's brazenness was now obvious – he thought he was hunting an unarmed man. Cutler was arrogant and overconfident, despite Hudson having bested him once already. He'd use Cutler's hubris against him again. Taking a deep breath, Hudson slid out from beneath cover, but kept the pistol hidden.

"You win," said Hudson, as Cutler locked eyes with his. "I give up." Cutler grinned, though Hudson hadn't finished, "But I need to let you into a little secret first."

"What secret is that, Mr. Powell?" said Cutler, strolling towards him with the casual menace of a corrupt jailer. "There's nothing you can know that I don't already."

"Then let me explain..." said Hudson, aiming the weapon at Cutler and squeezing the trigger. Cutler staggered back as the bullet hammered into his thigh – Hudson hadn't aimed to kill – and then dropped to one knee. However, incredibly, Cutler didn't fall, and Hudson couldn't see any blood.

Shit, his clothes must be armored, like Tory's! Hudson realized. He squeezed the trigger again, this time hitting Cutler on his back. The mercenary curled into a ball to protect his exposed head, yelping in pain as the second round struck. Wasting no time, Hudson vaulted the pillar and charged, driving his shoulder into Cutler as the mercenary staggered back to his feet. Cutler's weapon sailed from his hand, and clattered across the floor, followed soon after by Hudson's own body. The force of the impact had unbalanced him, and caused him to fall awkwardly. He shook his head and checked on Cutler, but the mercenary was still flat out. "Hudson two, Cutler nil, asshole..." he called out. But there was no time to gloat; he had to get back to Liberty, before Tory put a bullet in her.

Scrambling back to his feet, Hudson staggered towards the central sphere. He was still dazed from the collision with Cutler, but he'd managed to hold on to his pistol, which was still clasped tightly between his fingers. Hudson orbited the sphere and then slid to a stop as he caught up with Tory and Liberty. Both women were breathless and had their guards raised. Blood trickled from Liberty's nose, but Tory was also cut above the eye. Hudson aimed the weapon at Tory and edged to Liberty's side.

"Cutler's down, you can go now..." said Hudson, but the mercenary's eyes were still feral. "Tory, back off, it's over."

"This won't be over until one of you is dead," growled Tory, glancing over to Hudson. "You'll have to kill him."

Hudson shook his head, "You know I won't do that."

"Then this isn't over," Tory hit back, "and you'll force me to come after you again."

"That's up to you, Tory," replied Hudson, lowering his pistol. Then he turned to Liberty. "Come on, let's get out of here."

Hudson and Liberty slowly backed away from Tory, like safari explorers trying to escape from a wild animal. But then new voices bled into the room. Hudson stood still, scanning the different tunnel entrances, until he saw them. A group of four relic hunters had just entered the hexagonal space from a corridor directly behind Tory. They continued bantering between themselves until they saw Tory, and then Hudson and Liberty. Everyone froze, and in the silence that followed, Hudson could have heard a drop of his sweat splash on the metal floor. Then the relic hunter crew drew their weapons and the quiet was shattered like a twenty-one-gun salute.

CHAPTER 11

Tory was hit in the opening volley of rounds from the relic hunter crew. She went down, but Hudson didn't know how badly she was hurt. Hudson escaped the initial onslaught and ran for cover behind one of the metal beams, firing wildly in the direction of the hunter crew. He checked behind and saw that Liberty had slipped around the rear of the central sphere, possibly with the intent to flank the intruders. Then he glanced back at Tory, worried she might be bleeding out, but the mercenary had managed to drag herself behind another beam. She was holding her ribs, face twisted into an agonized grimace. He considered running to her, but the bell-like chime of bullets ringing off the beam next to his head convinced him otherwise.

"We don't have any relics!" Hudson shouted out, hoping to convince the rival crew that they weren't worth the effort. "We only just got here!"

"Drop your bags and your weapons, and we'll let you leave..." a rich, well-spoken voice called back.

"Why don't you come and get them, shit head." Tory shouted out, before Hudson could think of a response. Even so, Tory's retort would not have been his first choice.

Hudson chanced another look over the beam, and saw the four-person crew split into two groups of two. One duo – both young men, perhaps a little older than Liberty – ran to Hudson's right. This put them on a course to where Cutler still lay unconscious on the deck, and to where Liberty was circling around the back of the sphere. The other group was comprised of the baritone older man and a middle-aged woman with the stocky physique of a shot putter. They were moving more cautiously from beam to beam, working their way towards Hudson and Tory. Hudson knew it was a bad tactical situation; they were outnumbered and outgunned.

Tory was still cradling her ribs, but she was also now creeping along the line of the beam, towards the approaching pair. She clicked her fingers in rapid succession to get Hudson's attention and then pointed to something nearby. It was the antique single-action revolver, which was resting on the floor, far closer to Hudson than it was to Tory.

Don't do anything stupid, Hudson, don't do anything stupid... he told himself over and over in his head. However, the two other hunters were closing, and in a gun battle, two versus two were far better odds. Especially when one of those guns belonged to Tory Bellona.

Hudson steeled himself and then ran out from cover, firing in the direction of the two older hunters. Shots were returned, before the pair dove down out of sight. Reaching the revolver, he shoved it towards Tory with his foot, sending it spinning across the floor and into her waiting grasp. Shots rang out again and Hudson dropped to the deck and rolled behind the nearest beam. His heart was pumping so hard he felt like it would explode from his chest. The reality was that he'd literally just dodged a bullet.

Tory clicked back the hammer and then stood tall, before marching towards Hudson as if she was merely taking a morning stroll. For a moment, he worried that he was the intended target. However, as Tory reached Hudson's side, she just glanced over to him and said, "Go help your partner. These two are mine..."

If it had been anyone else speaking those words, Hudson would have laughed and told them not to be so stupid. However, this was Tory Bellona, and coming from her, Hudson only had sympathy for the two unfortunate hunters who had managed to piss her off.

Scrambling back to his feet, Hudson darted from cover to cover as the unmistakable report of a forty-five echoed around the room. Then he slid under one of the higher metal pillars and came face-to-face with the two younger relic hunters. Both Hudson and the hunters were startled, but Hudson reacted more quickly, slapping the closest man's weapon away. He then grabbed the hunter's jacket and wrestled him down.

Simultaneously, as if she'd been waiting for Hudson's arrival, Liberty vaulted a pillar, and kicked the second younger hunter in the back. The man recovered quickly and swung his weapon towards Liberty, but there was little commitment in his action, and Liberty was able to swoop in and disarm him easily.

"Wait, stop, I don't want to hurt you!" the young man cried out, but the pleads of mercy fell on deaf ears. Liberty landed a fierce three-step combo that put the man on his back. Hudson heard the crunch of cartilage, even over the rest of commotion. The second hunter had climbed to his knees just in time to witness Liberty's brutal display. The man watched his partner hit the floor like a sack of flour, briefly met Liberty's eyes, and then ran.

"Remind me never to piss you off," said Hudson, as the hunter scarpered.

Liberty smiled, but then the sound of more heavy boots filtered into the room. Liberty leaped up onto a nearby pillar and then turned back to Hudson, "It's the RGF!"

"Shit, come on!" Hudson called back, "If they catch us here, we'll be forced to pay for any damages, with money we don't have!"

Liberty jumped down from the pillar and ran to Hudson's side. Together they raced away from the approaching squad of RGF cops.

"Where do we go?" Liberty asked as they ran.

Hudson glanced back, counting five or six RGF officers at the far side of the room, creeping slowly towards them. "I don't know... just pick a tunnel and keep running."

Liberty darted left and accelerated, but then noticed that Hudson wasn't with her and slid to a stop. "Where the hell are you going?!"

"I'll catch you up!" Hudson called out, heading towards where he'd last seen Tory. "Go, I won't be long."

Liberty cursed, and then picked up speed, "Damn it, Hudson, that woman is going to be the death of you!"

Maybe... Hudson thought, as he vaulted a pillar, and raced on. *But, if I don't warn her about the RGF, she'll probably skin me alive...*

Hudson reached the location where he'd kicked Tory's revolver back to her and saw someone on the floor, face down. "Tory!" he called out, and then slid down by the side of the body. However, it was immediately apparent that it wasn't Tory. Flipping the body onto its back, Hudson saw that it was the stocky female hunter. Hudson felt for a pulse, but there was none, and then he noticed the hole in her chest, right above her heart.

"You need to get out of here."

Hudson looked up and saw Tory, blood smeared down her face and neck, casually reloading her revolver. Hudson sprang up at her side, and then spotted another body, lying motionless on the ground about ten meters away.

"You killed them both?" said Hudson, phrasing it as a question, though he already knew the answer.

"Yes," said Tory, coolly, as she closed the cylinder of the six-shooter. However Tory must have seen the disappointment etched into the lines on Hudson's brow, and added, "They attacked us, Hudson. This isn't a game. It's kill or be killed."

"You're right," replied Hudson, trying to put the bodies out of his mind. It was true that the rival crew had attacked them, but he still wished Tory had found a non-lethal response. *Maybe I'm just being naïve...* Hudson thought. *In a dog-eat-dog world, surely it's better to be the dog that doesn't get eaten...* The shouts of the RGF squad snapped his focus back to Tory and their predicament. Hudson reached out and held Tory by the shoulders. She flinched momentarily, startled by Hudson's touch, but didn't pull away. "You need to run too," he urged her, "a whole squad of RGF just arrived; we have maybe a couple of minutes before they find us in here!"

"I can't leave Cutler," said Tory firmly, while holstering the revolver.

"Damn it, Tory, what is it with that guy?" protested Hudson. "The RGF will charge you for the damage in here; is he worth that? Why the hell are you so loyal to him?" It was the last part, more than any other, that really irked Hudson.

This time Tory did step back, shrugging off Hudson's hold on her shoulders as she did so. "We can afford the hit," she said, ignoring Hudson's probes into her relationship with Cutler. "Now get the hell out of here, while you still can."

Hudson was about to argue back, but then from the gloom the younger relic hunter that had run from Liberty emerged. He saw the body of the woman on the deck and his face twisted into a ghoulish mix of anger and grief.

"You killed her!" he yelled, raising his weapon at Tory. His hand was shaking and tears were starting to cloud his vision.

Tory slowly moved her hand to the grip of her revolver again, but she did not draw it. "Yes, I killed her," she said, meeting the relic hunter's eyes. Her tone was dispassionate and matter-of-fact. "And the man too; your father, I'm guessing? What exactly did you expect to happen when you started shooting at us?"

"You murdered them!" the man yelled, tears now streaming down his face.

"There's no murder in here, boy," Tory hit back. Hudson could hear the malice in her voice; this was the side of Tory he hated and feared. "There is just survival."

Thanks to her reinforced clothing, Hudson knew that Tory could take a bullet – he'd even shot her once himself – but the young relic hunter would not be so fortunate. And there was still a chance that Tory could get shot somewhere the armor couldn't protect. He made a split-second decision, knowing even in that fractional amount of time that it was a foolish choice. He stepped out in front of the hunter, putting his own body between Tory and the weapon, and held his arms out wide. "It's over, kid," Hudson said, aware his voice was shaky, "No-one else needs to die."

"Get out of my way," the man howled back, trying to aim around Hudson, but he was shielding Tory completely from view. "You knew the risks coming in here," Hudson continued, taking another pace towards him. "We all knew the risks. Shooting her won't change that. It just makes you a killer too."

Hudson could see the young hunter's resolve was wavering. Despite the tears, he could see it in the man's eyes. They were not the eyes of a killer.

The man lowered the weapon. "I told them not to attack..." he said, forcing the words out through barely-restrained sobs. "I told them..."

Hudson moved in and stripped the weapon from the hunter's hand. He wanted to offer the young man some comfort – some words of consolation – but there were no words, and there was also no time. The RGF squad was creeping ever closer, and he had to get away. If the RGF caught him, he'd end up in a cell on some crappy penal station for being unable to pay the RGF's fine.

Leaning closer to the young hunter, Hudson said, "You have to go, now, or they'll catch us both. Run, and don't look back." The man glanced beyond Hudson, presumably to Tory, whose presence Hudson could still feel, like sunlight on his back. Then he met Hudson's eyes again, before he span on his heels and started to run.

Hudson breathed a sigh of relief, but then he heard the tell-tale click-click-click-click of a revolver's hammer being drawn back. He turned and confronted Tory, putting his body between the barrel of her revolver and the fleeing relic hunter. Out of the corner of his eyes, he could see the flickering shapes of the RGF officers. They had sixty seconds to get away, maybe less.

"Get out of the way, Hudson," demanded Tory. He could see that his actions had given her pause, but there was still fire burning behind Tory's eyes, and Hudson knew he could easily get burned.

"Let him go, Tory," replied Hudson, tossing the hunter's weapon to the floor and holstering his own. "You've already won."

Tory shook her head, "You still don't get it, do you?" she hit back, talking down to Hudson in the same way Griff always used to. "There is no honor amongst thieves. There's no mercy, not inside these wrecks."

"There is while I'm here," said Hudson, standing tall. He wasn't going to allow Tory to give in to her baser instincts. Despite her actions, he had to believe there was something more to her than a callous killer. He had to believe she wasn't the same as Cutler Wendell.

Tory took two paces forward, standing so close that Hudson could feel the warmth of her breath. "That hunter will be back," she said, softly, though the words still dripped with menace. "If not today, some other day. All your noble deed does is delay his revenge."

"Not everyone is like Cutler Wendell," said Hudson, holding his ground, despite Tory's intimidating proximity. "You can still choose. You can still come with me."

Tory raised her revolver and stroked a line down Hudson's cheek with the tip of the barrel. She then leaned in so close that her hair brushed against Hudson's cheek. A shiver ran down his spine; he didn't know whether she was going to kiss him or kill him, assuming the anticipation didn't slay him first. Then Tory de-cocked the revolver and whispered into his ear, "You're playing a very dangerous game, Hudson Powell. Be sure you are willing to finish what you start." She then drew back and holstered the revolver. "It's time you left."

Hudson had almost forgotten about the RGF squad, but they were now practically on top of them.

"You two, halt!" cried one of the officers.

Hudson glanced over to the squad, fixing their positions in his mind, before turning back to Tory. "I'll see you again soon," he said, and then he ran, harder and faster than he'd ever run in his life.

"Hey, stop!" he heard a voice shout, and he gritted his teeth, half-expecting shots to ring out after him. However, there was only the sound of the air rushing past his face. Hudson spotted the corridor he'd seen Liberty head towards and adjusted his course, legs and lungs burning from the exertion. He slowed and ducked inside the tunnel, which was smaller than the usual hexagonal openings. A few hurried paces inside the gloomy, cramped space, he collided with something solid, and bit down hard to avoid crying out in pain. Hudson tried to maneuver himself around the object, but the corridor was growing darker, making progress more difficult.

"Liberty!" he shouted out in a hushed, but urgent call. "Liberty, are you in here?" There was a faint reply, but he couldn't quite place its location. Pushing on, stumbling over yet more unseen obstacles, Hudson called out again. His lights were still in his rucksack, and he considered stopping to dig one out, but then he heard Liberty's voice calling back. It was still distant, but clearer than before; he was getting closer. He pressed on through the encroaching darkness, calling out again and again, until his foot failed to land on solid metal. He stumbled forward and slipped. The next thing he knew he was falling, only for a second, before his body hammered into a solid wall, rebounding him along another corridor, like a marble falling through a marble run. He bounced off another surface and then was sliding, faster and faster, unable to stop himself. Fear and panic gripped him as he tried desperately to arrest his fall, until he finally landed on something soft and rolled out into a dimly lit room. Rubbing his head, he groaned from the multiple bumps and scrapes he'd suffered during the plunge, and attempted to take stock of his new location.

Suddenly, Liberty's face appeared above him, a torchlight strapped to her head. Hudson shielded his eyes from the glare. "There you are; I heard you shouting, but I couldn't make out what you were saying."

Liberty rolled her eyes, but then, unexpectedly, laughed. "I was trying to warn you not to come any closer, or you might fall and get trapped down here with me..."

"Oh..." said Hudson, as he pushed himself to a sitting position and rubbed his aching muscles. "That was pretty good advice."

Liberty smiled, "Uh huh... But, seeing as though you're here now, you can help me find a way out."

CHAPTER 12

In addition to the torchlight strapped to her head, Liberty had also set up a small lamp in the corner of the room. It was like having a log fire burning inside a dusty, old study. And although the lamp didn't flicker as firelight would, its dim illumination still created an eerie atmosphere. Hudson got up and brushed the dust off his pants. Remarkably, considering how far and how quickly he'd fallen, he didn't feel too bad.

"I'm glad I landed on something soft," he said, removing his pack and searching for his own headtorch. "I wouldn't fancy trying to climb back out of here with a broken arm or leg."

Liberty laughed again, "I think our new friend here agrees."

Hudson scowled and then looked behind him to see the skeletal remains of a hunter squashed on the floor. "Oh, shit!" Hudson yelled, jumping back as if he'd just seen a giant spider. "Damn it, Liberty, why didn't you warn me?!" he asked, however Liberty was still too busy finding Hudson's evident discomfort amusing to reply.

"It's just an old skeleton," said Liberty, after her giggles had subsided. "Haven't you seen a skeleton before?"

Hudson's brow furrowed even more deeply, "Well, of course not. Why the hell have you seen a skeleton before?" Then he realized he'd rather not know the answer. "Actually, don't tell me, I really don't want to know."

"You should be thanking our bony friend," said Liberty, "his rucksack and bedroll is what cushioned your fall. Unfortunately for him, it seems that there was no padding in place when he fell in here."

Hudson went over to inspect the remains. He was no expert in decomposition, but the bones were dry, which even he knew meant that they had probably been there for many years. He gingerly pulled the dead man's rucksack towards him, dislodging the skeleton's shoulder as he did so. This caused Hudson's face to twist into a sickened grimace and Liberty to laugh. He opened the bag and cautiously began to rummage around inside.

"This room was once part of a larger space," said Liberty, tapping her knuckles against a crumpled wall nearby. "It perhaps buckled when the ship crashed onto the planet," she added, while Hudson carefully emptied the contents of the dead hunter's rucksack onto the floor. "I haven't found a way out yet, but I'll continue to scout for exits, while you rob old skellybobs, there."

Hudson shot Liberty a dirty look. "Have a bit of respect, will you? This was a person at one time, just like you and me."

"And I have no desire to end up like him," said Liberty, more seriously. "Think about it – he died here, alone, injured and in the dark. I'm not going out like that."

Hudson shuddered at the thought of it; Liberty's description painted a pretty bleak picture. "Don't worry, there are two of us, and we still have all our gear. We'll find a way out, even if it means climbing back the way we came in."

"Whatever you say, skipper," said Liberty, continuing to inspect the walls for any possible collapsed exits. "Let me know if you find anything exciting." Hudson laughed, causing Liberty to shoot a curious glance back at him. "Is that a funny ha-ha, laugh, or a nervous, we-are-going-to-die laugh?" she asked.

Hudson held up a fistful of alien relics, which included a high-grade CPU shard. "It's a, 'this guy had a decent score' laugh."

Liberty rushed over and dropped to her knees at Hudson's side, excitedly examining the alien components that her partner had discovered.

"There's some good stuff here," she said, grouping them on the floor. She then pointed to each little collection in turn. "This guy knew his alien components, that's for sure. There are super-conducting thermoelectric generators, broad-spectrum sensors, a bunch of components that are essential for high-end astrionics systems, and that high-grade CPU shard, of course."

Hudson picked up the CPU shard, while Liberty busily packed the most valuable items into her own rucksack. The shard was similar to the relic he'd auctioned back on Earth, and alone might be enough to cover the remaining balance of the VCX-110. "Looks like our little trip down here was a lucky break," said Hudson, slipping the CPU shard into the shielded compartment in his jacket. "This wreck would have mostly been cleaned out of top-grade components like these decades ago."

Liberty finished packing and closed the flap on the rucksack. "Sadly for this guy, that's probably how long he's been here," she commented, looking down at the remains of the dead hunter.

Then Hudson noticed something poking out from a small rip in the dead hunter's rucksack. He checked back inside, but the bag was empty. "That's odd," he said out loud, drawing another curious look from Liberty. He returned to the exterior of the bag and dug his finger inside the tear, ripping it wider to reveal a hidden compartment. "Well, I'll be damned," he said, reaching inside.

"I'll be damned, what?" asked Liberty, shuffling closer.

Hudson smiled and pulled out a small object, about the size of a champagne cork. It shone with an alien, almost metallic hue. He turned it over and over between his fingers, while both of them stared at it in rapt attention.

"Is that what I think it is?" asked Liberty.

Hudson reached inside the hidden compartment in his jacket and pulled out the alien crystal shard. Slowly, and as tentatively as if the object was an explosive charge, he drew the two crystals closer. At about an inch distant, the smaller relic snapped out of Hudson's fingers and latched on to the top of the larger object. They created a seamless, whole crystal; it was as if the two relics had never been parted.

"Yep, I think it is..." said Hudson.

CHAPTER 13

Hudson examined the newly completed alien crystal for a few more seconds, momentarily entranced by its hypnotic beauty. He then held it out to Liberty. "Here, take this while I see if there's anything else hidden in this guy's rucksack." Liberty hesitated briefly, but then tentatively accepted the crystal off Hudson. She cradled the relic, as reverently as if it were the long-lost Florentine Diamond.

"I can't believe we've found the missing piece," Liberty said, shining the beam of her headtorch directly onto the crystal. The light reflected and refracted, creating a mesmerizing cascade of colors and patterns in the room.

Hudson was again busying himself searching inside the newly-revealed secret compartment. His fingers touched on another object, and he slowly removed what turned out to be a small leather wallet. "Maybe this guy had some notion of what the crystal is," he said, unfolding the wallet gently and setting out the contents on the floor. "If we can figure that out, we may just become the richest rookie relic hunters in the galaxy."

"Speaking of riches," said Liberty, as she spotted a clip of hardbucks. She picked it up and removed the wedge of cash, before quickly counting it. "Twelve hundred and fifty," she said, wafting the notes at Hudson. His eyes lit up and reached for the stack, but Liberty drew it back before his fingers could close around the notes. "I'll look after these," she said, in an almost motherly tone, "Just to make sure you don't drink it all away."

Hudson scowled, and then watched as Liberty lowered the zip of her jacket about half-way. She slid the wedge of notes inside, before zipping the jacket back up again. "Where the hell did you just hide them?"

"None of your business," Liberty replied, snootily. Hudson laughed, "So long as you can get at them to buy me a drink, without exposing yourself, I don't give a damn."

"Charming..." replied Liberty, with the same snootiness. Then she reached down and picked up an ID card from the pile, similar to their own relic hunter licenses. "Percy Harrison," she said, reading the name on the card. Hudson looked up with a confused frown; he hadn't noticed that Liberty had taken the card. "That's our deceased friend, here.

Percy Harrison was his name." She held the card out to Hudson, "Good-looking guy; at one time, anyway. Not so much now..."

Hudson snorted a laugh, "I think whether or not he was a 'good-looking guy' is fairly low down the list of things we need to understand about him."

"Sure, because you're definitely not one to have your eye turned by an attractive relic hunter..." Liberty hit back.

"Returning to help Tory was a purely business decision," said Hudson, refusing to be goaded. "As long as Tory Bellona is disinclined to murder us, we're far more likely to survive future encounters with Cutler Wendell."

"Whatever you say, skipper," Liberty replied, sounding distinctly unconvinced. She then placed the ID back on the pile and picked up a small black notebook. "Hey, this guy took notes with actual handwriting."

"People do still write with pen and paper, you know?" said Hudson, shaking his head.

"Yeah, and I suppose they chisel words into stone tablets too..."

Hudson paused sorting through the items in the wallet, most of which were of no value or interest, and shot Liberty a wearied look. "You could do something useful and actually read that notebook," he said. He then added with a wry smile, "Assuming reading isn't also too archaic a pastime for you?"

Liberty gently set the crystal down on the ground, before opening the notebook on the first page. "Once upon a time, in a galaxy far, far away, there was a dashing young relic hunter, called Percy Harrison..." Hudson laughed and smiled at Liberty, but didn't interrupt. "He fell down a shaft and died. The end."

"Riveting..." said Hudson, packing up the contents of the wallet again.

Then Liberty's eyes narrowed and her mirthful expression disappeared. "Wow, wait a minute..." she said, "Listen to this..." Hudson sat up in anticipation and waited for Liberty to continue. "My continued search of the alien wreck on Brahms Three has come up negative once again," she read out-loud from the notebook. "The larger crystalline piece that fell from my rucksack while fleeing from a rival hunter crew remains lost. My only hope now is to return to Bach Two, and again scour that wreck for the smaller half's original counterpart. I do not hold out much hope. Of the thirty-five wrecks I have explored, I have found intact crystals on only these two vessels. On all of the wrecks where I was able to reach the crystal chamber, only shattered fragments remained."

Liberty stopped reading and for several seconds they both digested what they'd learned.

"He mentioned a crystal chamber," said Hudson, breaking the silence. "Does he say anything more about what that is, or where it might be? Maybe it could help us understand what this thing is."

Liberty nodded and started to scan ahead, flipping page after page until she stopped and began to read again.

"I regret that I have still learned little about the function of the crystal. Without the larger half, I fear I will never understand its secrets. It is like trying to hear music, but with most of the notes missing and no idea what the melody should sound like. However, my tests so far suggest that, while its signature is unique, it is also able to resonate at the same frequency as the portals. Several times while transitioning through a portal the crystal has exhibited a behavior that I simply cannot explain. It is possible that a fully intact crystal could even manipulate the portals or perhaps communicate through them. In fact, the crystal chambers may be the communications centers of these great alien vessels. The Broca area, if you will. It is possible these chambers were even located inside the vessel's main command and control center. Though, besides a unique pod-like structure that, despite my efforts, I was unable to open, I found nothing else that could confirm this hypothesis."

Hudson frowned. "The Broca area?"

"It's a part of the brain linked to speech," said Liberty, without hesitation. Then she appeared to notice Hudson's shocked, wide-eyed response and added, "I don't just know about engines and starships, you know..."

Hudson responded with a cheeky, 'hark at you' face, but then he suddenly remembered something and clicked his fingers excitedly. "Wait, the assessor I had examine the crystal on Earth also suggested it could be some kind of transceiver. He said it might unlock the possibility for near instant communication between portal worlds. He also suggested that it may perhaps have the ability to manipulate the portals."

Liberty whistled, "If that were true then it would certainly make it incredibly valuable."

Hudson picked up the crystal and placed it back inside the hidden compartment in his jacket. "Come on, let's get out of here," he said, standing up and inspecting the hole through which they both fell. "Thanks to Percy, I already think we have a big enough score, and I'd rather avoid another encounter with Cutler, if we can help it." Then he looked back at Liberty and noticed she seemed sullen. "Hey, what's up?

Liberty stood up, still holding the notebook. "I guess this was like his diary," she said, softly. "There's one final entry."

Hudson felt his mouth go dry; he knew what was coming.

Liberty cleared her throat and read from the little black book again. "The infection in my leg has grown out of control and fever has taken hold. My medical supplies are gone. It was foolish of me not to replenish my stocks before I embarked on this hunt. My eagerness to find the crystal fragment made me careless, and now I will never discover the truth. Worse, I have run out of water and the power cells in my lamps are almost gone. I fear I will die here in the cold, empty darkness of this alien space. I fear I will die alone. But more than that, I fear that I will have died for nothing."

Liberty closed the notepad and a solemn silence followed. Hudson looked down at the body of Percy Harrison and felt his pain almost as keenly as if it were his own. He too had felt loneliness and despair, but his pain paled in comparison to what this unfortunate relic hunter must have faced. Hudson had discovered a renewed purpose to his life. And he'd found someone to share it with. Whether or not he was able to uncover the secrets of the newly re-forged crystal, he already knew that he was a wealthier man than the one lying at his feet.

He looked over at Liberty and placed a hand gently on her shoulder, "Come on, Liberty. Let's go back to Earth."

CHAPTER 14

Getting themselves out of the room that had accidentally become Percy Harrison's tomb had not been straightforward. Were it not for their newly-acquired climbing gear, they may well have ended up as permanent residents, alongside the unfortunate ex-relic hunter. In particular, the self-attaching pitons that Tory had tossed into Hudson's trolley in the Scavenger's Paradise had been literal life-savers. Once again Hudson found himself indebted to the mysterious woman who had been hired to kill him.

Thankfully, the remainder of the journey back out of the wreck had been far less eventful than their excursion inside. The strange, shallow room with the central sphere and many pillars was now deathly quiet. The RGF squad and the bodies of the hunters that Tory had killed were all gone. And, other than the occasional spent ammo casing, it would have been impossible to tell that anyone had entered the space in decades.

Without the map, which Hudson had dropped during the chaos of the earlier skirmish, it had taken a few wrong turns to find their way to the exit. But, almost three hours after starting their ascent from the tomb, they eventually emerged from the wreck. After so long spent in the murky depths of the alien vessel, the sunlight was almost blinding, and it took Hudson's eyes a few minutes to adjust. However, it wasn't only the piercing sunlight that he needed time to adjust to. He also needed a few minutes to fully take in everything that had happened.

"I think I'd call that a successful first hunt," said Hudson, resting his back on the railings of the platform outside the wreck entrance. It was raining, as it did most of the year on Bach Two, and Hudson held his head back, allowing the cooling droplets to soothe his tired face.

Liberty cocked an eyebrow, "I'm not sure I agree with your definition of successful. We almost died – three times."

"Almost..." said Hudson, wiping the rain from his eyes and smiling back at her. "Any hunt where you don't die is a good one, I'd say. Besides, we got out with a bag full of alien relics, and we're another step closer to learning what the crystal is."

Liberty nodded and half-shrugged at the same time, evidently finding it hard to argue with

Hudson's assessment. However, she then stiffened up, and anxiously started to check around them, as if expecting to be jumped on at any moment. "Do you think Cutler and Tory are still here?"

In the struggle to escape the wreck, and the relief of stepping back out into the open air again, Hudson had forgotten about the two mercenaries. He instinctively reached for the compact pistol in his shoulder holster, and felt reassured knowing it was still there.

"That's a good question, and one I can't answer," said Hudson. "We've been gone for several hours. And if the RGF squad did arrest and charge them for damaging the wreck, it's likely they would have been banned from entering the checkpoint district." Then he shrugged, "For a few days, at least."

Liberty frowned, and joined Hudson leaning against the balcony railings. The rain softly pattered against the tough fabric of her new relic hunter's jacket. Then she tilted her head to the side and glanced up at Hudson. "You don't sound entirely convinced..."

"I'm not," admitted Hudson. "Anyone with connections to someone as shady as Logan Griff probably has other shady friends too. I doubt Cutler would have survived this long without being able to talk, muscle or bribe his way out of worse situations." Hudson suddenly had a compelling urge to leave the planet. The more he thought about Cutler and Griff, the more it felt like they were lurking just around the next corner.

"Come on, let's declare our score and get it auctioned off on-site. We'll need the credits to pay the taxes to the RGF and the CET, and to buy our ticket back to Earth."

They made their way down the many staircases that ran parallel to the hull of the wreck until they reached the soft, slightly squelchy turf of Bach Two. The rain had started to come down harder, reducing their visibility. It made Hudson feel even more anxious about who might be up ahead. Cautiously, they proceeded to the checkpoint scanners and waited in the short line until their turn came.

"Place any relics that you need to declare onto the conveyor and then step through the scanner," said a miserable looking RGF officer. Rainwater was running off his cap like it was a leaky gutter. "Any items you fail to declare will be picked up by the body scanner and confiscated by the RGF."

Hudson nodded to Liberty, and she began to empty the relics from her rucksack into a wide, gray-colored plastic tray. As she was doing this another RGF officer approached, wearing his hood up to protect against the rain. He tapped the officer at the checkpoint scanner on the shoulder, and the two stepped away. They spoke for a few moments, beyond the earshot of Hudson. Though the driving rain made it difficult to hear anything other than water crashing against his leather jacket. Then the first officer simply moved over to man the adjacent checkpoint scanner, without offering an explanation. Hudson felt a shiver run down his spine; he could feel something was off. He slid his hand just inside his jacket, ready to draw the pistol, if needed. Then the newly-arrived RGF officer threw back his hood, and Hudson's hand fell limply to his side.

"Hello, rook," said Logan Griff, with a smile that made Hudson's stomach churn. "I told you I'd find you."

"What do you want, Griff?" said Hudson, trying to sound tough, even though it was clear what Griff wanted. "I'm a licensed relic hunter now. I have every right to be here."

Liberty appeared at Hudson's side, having finished emptying their score into the plastic tray. She looked first at Hudson, whose stare remained fixed on Logan Griff, and then to the RGF officer.

Griff's sodden mustache twitched as he met Liberty's eyes. He then wiped his fingers around the corners of his mouth as he looked her up and down, not even attempting to hide how blatantly he was checking her out. "I see you still haven't learned a damn thing, rook," said Griff, continuing to gawk at Liberty. "How long before you get this pretty little one killed too? I should just put her out of her misery now."

Liberty took a step towards Griff, "Why don't you come and try it, shit head," she snarled at him. Hudson was quick to step between them, putting his back towards Griff as he did so. "Take it easy, Liberty," said Hudson, in a hushed voice so only Liberty could hear. "Don't give him a reason. He could put you in a cell just for the threat alone. Inside the checkpoint district, the RGF have all the power."

Liberty looked up at him, rain streaming down her cheeks like tears, "But Hudson, we can't just let him..."

"We don't have a choice, Liberty," Hudson interrupted. "There will be other opportunities. Other hunts. This isn't over."

Liberty's eyes fell to the mud beneath her boots. Hudson wanted to say more, but he didn't want to give Griff the satisfaction of seeing him console his partner. Instead, he turned to face his former training officer and stood tall. "Just get on with it, Griff. We all know why you're here."

Griff grinned again, and then walked over to the plastic tray of relics. "I'm afraid due to a violation of RGF code..." he then paused and pressed a finger to his temple, as if pretending to be deep in thought, "Five, Seven, Alpha... something... something..." he said, and then laughed at his own cruel joke. "I hereby confiscate these relics." Griff then rummaged through the contents of the tray, before picking out a couple of super-conducting thermoelectric generators. He placed one into the top pocket of his coat, grinning even more nauseatingly at Hudson as he did so. Then, unexpectedly, he threw one high into the air behind them. Hudson and Liberty both spun around and saw the alien relic sail into the outstretched hands of Cutler Wendell.

Due to the clatter of the driving rain, and Logan Griff's off-putting, sudden appearance, he hadn't heard Cutler sneak up on them. And, as the mercenary stepped closer, Hudson could see that he wasn't alone – Tory was just behind him. That she was still at his side angered Hudson almost as much as getting ripped off by Griff.

Liberty again darted forward, face twisted with rage, but Hudson caught her arm and held her back. His intervention was not a second too soon, as Cutler had already reached down and placed his hand on his weapon.

"Liberty, don't," said Hudson, more urgently. "Getting yourself killed won't help us get even."

"We're not even close to even," said Cutler, tossing the relic back to Tory. She caught it and placed it into the pocket of her armored jacket, holding Hudson's eyes as she did so. "You'd better be watching your back, every hour of every day from now on, Hudson Powell," Cutler continued. "Because I'm never going to stop coming for you."

Griff tipped the remainder of the tray's contents into a black satchel and then walked around the side of the Shaak radiation detector. He made an elaborate show of doing so, making sure that Hudson had seen him do it. Griff's unspoken message was clear – the entire score was going directly into the pockets of the RGF. Straight to Chief Inspector Jane Wash. And Griff had already taken his slice.

"You may now pass through the detector," said Griff, waving them on, as if conducting them into a gala ball.

Hudson walked through, defiantly, and then stood in front of Griff with his arms held wide. "Happy? Or do you want to frisk me first?"

"I think I'll save that for your pretty little partner," said Griff, wiping the corner of his mouth again. "And I'll only be happy when I'm standing over your cold, dead corpse." Then he looked at Liberty and smiled, "Come on, dumb rook junior," he said, waving her through.

Liberty looked ready to rip Griff's throat out, but she held her nerve and paced through the detector as defiantly as Hudson had done. And, as with Hudson, the Shaak detector picked up nothing. However, unlike Hudson, Liberty didn't hold her arms out. She simply stood there, fists clenched so tightly that even the driving rain couldn't seep in.

Griff moved in front of Liberty and checked her out again, as obviously as he had done before. "Are you sure you haven't got anything hidden inside that snug little jacket of yours?" he said, leering down at her. "Maybe I should search you, just to be sure?"

Liberty took a step towards Griff, making Hudson flinch, worried for what she might do, but somehow, Liberty kept a lid on her fury.

"Touch me, and I will break you apart, asshole" said Liberty, glaring back at Griff. "Try it. Please..."

Hudson had met some menacing folk on his journeys, few more so than Cutler Wendell and Tory Bellona. However, in that moment, he doubted he'd seen anything more chillingly sinister than Liberty's hateful glower at Logan Griff. Even Griff seemed to feel its menace, and he backed off, holding up his hands in surrender. Though, the sleazy smile never left his lips.

"You two idiots are free to go," said Griff, glancing back at Hudson. "And good luck on your next hunt. I'll enjoy taking that from you too."

Hudson had nothing more to say; he feared that if he opened his mouth, he'd just say something he'd regret. They'd lost their score, but still had their lives, and their freedom, if only so that Griff and his cronies could rob them again in the future. But being able to walk free was still a victory, and more than he had expected. He turned and strode away, nodding to Liberty to follow. She waited for a second and then barged past Griff, knocking him back a couple of paces, before quickly reaching Hudson's side.

For several minutes Hudson and Liberty walked in silence, until they reached the border gate to the scavenger town. Then, once they were inside, Liberty let out a primal scream, and kicked over a stack of empty containers that had been piled up behind one of the commercial buildings.

"Liberty, it's okay..." Hudson began, but Liberty was in no mood to be placated.

"It's not okay, Hudson," she yelled. "We have nothing. No relics, no credits, and no ticket back to Earth. All we have is about fourteen hundred hardbucks. That will barely last us a week. And then what? How is any of this okay?"

Hudson moved to her side and then ushered her down the backstreet behind the commercial building. "Look, Griff thinks I'm an idiot," Hudson began. Liberty's eyebrows raised up, but he didn't allow her the chance to take a cheap shot at him. "Because of that, he didn't bother to search me." Hudson reached inside the shielded compartment in his jacket and pulled out the high-grade CPU shard he'd stashed there while inside the wreck. Suddenly Liberty's eyes softened, and she stopped pacing up and down the street like a mad person. "We're still in business, Liberty."

Liberty looked at the shard and then at Hudson, and she burst out laughing. It was a pure, unfiltered sound of joy that filled Hudson with happiness.

"What do you say we go and buy ourselves a ship?" said Hudson.

Liberty charged at Hudson and flung her arms around him. "Whatever you say, skipper."

CHAPTER 15

With a bit of creative negotiating, Hudson had managed to barter passage back to Earth for himself and Liberty on the next transport out. They didn't have enough hardbucks for two standard tickets, but there were always people who valued the untraceable nature of physical currency, above its actual dollar value. In this case, one of the ground crew at Bach Two's spaceport was willing to smuggle them on board through the cargo section, in return for a hefty wedge of notes.

This time, Hudson had taken no chances on the flight back. Despite their names not appearing on the official passenger manifest, he still didn't put it past the abilities of Griff or Cutler to find out they were on board. Hudson had already noted that Cutler's ship had departed Bach Two a few hours before they had. But that didn't mean that both Cutler and Tory were on board. The mercenaries may have scored a victory against them outside the alien wreck, but as Cutler had highlighted in no uncertain terms, there was still a score to settle. However, after a thorough search of all the passenger quarters and even crew sections, there was no sign of either of them. Hudson had secretly wished that Tory Bellona had been waiting for him on board. He'd had to force himself to wipe such sordid thoughts from his mind. As much as she didn't act like it, Tory was still under contract to kill him, and couldn't be trusted.

Hudson and Liberty stepped out of the taxi flyer that had flown them from Ride Spaceport to San Francisco. Hudson leant back in through the window and clasped hands with Nadia Voss.

"Thanks again for the ride, Nadia," he said. "This is becoming a bit of a habit."

Nadia smiled, "So long as you're making a habit of staying alive, I don't mind."

Liberty squeezed in beside Hudson at the passenger-side window, still wearing her relic hunting outfit, and dropped their remaining hardbucks onto the seat. Nadia shook her head and was about to return the money, but Liberty held up her hand. "I know you don't want it, but I insist," said Liberty. She had listened to the flyer pilot and Hudson chat during the ride over. During the course of their relaxed banter, it had become clear that Nadia had helped Hudson to escape from Cutler and Tory in the past. This was the maneuver they had referred to as 'the switcheroo'. "If it wasn't for you, Hudson would have never made it to San Francisco, and then we'd never have met."

Nadia laughed, "Surely, I should be apologizing for that, not being thanked?"

"Ha ha ha," said Hudson, in a forced, almost robotic-sounding tone.

"Take the hardbucks," said Liberty again. "It's the least we can do."

Nadia sighed and collected up the notes, before tapping them into a neat pile and placing them into her jacket pocket.

"You're going to split that with Dex, right?" asked Hudson, with a knowing smile.

Nadia looked shocked at the subtle implication that she was going to keep it for herself. "Of course! Not all of us are scoundrel, ex-clobber relic hunters, like you ..." Hudson conceded her point, graciously, but they were both smiling. "So, where are you two headed now?" Nadia then asked.

"We've got a ship to buy!" replied Liberty, unable to contain her excitement.

"But first, we need to make a trade," added Hudson, aware that Liberty was getting ahead of herself a little.

"Well, good luck out there," said Nadia, as her screen flashed up that another fare was waiting nearby. Then she looked at Liberty and added,

"Take care of him, will you? He's prone to making some pretty dumb choices."

"Hey!" protested Hudson, but Nadia and Liberty both ignored him.

"Though you seem to be the exception," Nadia went on.

"I will," said Liberty. "Besides, I can't ditch him now – I need him to fly my ship."

Nadia and Liberty both laughed, but Hudson shook his head. "I am still here, you know?"

"Take care Hudson Powell and Liberty Devan, relic hunters..." said Nadia, throwing up a salute.

Hudson and Liberty backed away from the taxi flyer and waved it off as it circled around them and headed off for its next job.

"Nice to see you do at least have *some* good taste in friends," said Liberty, nudging Hudson in the ribs.

Hudson knew that she was referring to Tory, but didn't take the bait.

"So, what's this trade you talked about?" Liberty added. "I don't know why you just didn't auction off the CPU shard on Bach Two."

"The exchange rate on Bach Two was pretty crappy," answered Hudson. "If we're going to make enough credits from this single CPU shard, our only choice is to move it via one of the bigger black-market dealers." He pressed his hand to the outside of his jacket, feeling the bumps of the crystal and CPU shard to make sure they were still safely hidden. "I'd rather not use this particular asshole, but we need to get the maximum value out of this CPU shard, and I have a feeling he'll be compliant."

Liberty shot him a curious glance. "That sounds ominous. But, so long as it's not someone else who wants to kill you, I don't really care." Hudson's reassuring response was conspicuous by its absence, so Liberty pressed him. "It isn't someone who's trying to kill you, right?"

Hudson shrugged, "No. Well, not anymore."

"Not anymore?!" Liberty repeated, the pitch of her voice rising to a level that only dogs could hear.

Hudson smiled at her, "Relax, it will be fine. And besides, I have you to protect me."

Liberty shook her head, "Yeah, but who's going to protect you from me..."

CHAPTER 16

Hudson pushed open the door to the Antiques and Curiosity Shoppe and walked in, with Liberty trailing close behind. A little bell rang out as the door closed again, and Hudson heard the voice of Cortland call out from somewhere in the back-office, shouting, "I won't be a moment!"

Hudson waited by the counter and popped open the strap on his shoulder holster, ready to draw the pistol should Cortland not be pleased to see him again. Liberty, meanwhile, started to study the wide variety of objects on the shelves, which ranged from alien relics to items from Earth's antiquity. She stopped at a shelf containing a damaged communications unit from an old CET military patrol craft. Hudson could tell from the look of concentration on her face that the device had given her an idea.

Liberty then rummaged through another three shelves, all containing a variety of common alien components. She appeared to be making a mental shopping list. Liberty was about to inspect the CET communications unit more closely when, like a magpie, something shiny caught her eye on a shelf lower down. She crouched to get a better look, and then her mouth arced into a wide smile. She was looking at an old Royal Air Force cap badge, dating from the second world war.

Hudson watched as Liberty picked up the badge and rubbed it gently between her finger and thumb, enthralled by it. He remembered how her old coveralls, which had fallen out of favor since acquiring the sleeker new relic hunter clothes, had also born the RAF name. He smiled, knowing that, no matter what deal was struck in the next few minutes, the cap badge would be a part of the package.

Cortland then bustled out from the back-office room, snapping Hudson's attention back to the matter at hand. "Sorry to keep you...", he said cheerfully. Then he spotted Hudson and he fell silent; the color draining from his cheeks.

"Take it easy, I'm not here to cause trouble," said Hudson. He was watching closely for any sign that Cortland might reach for his stun pistol, or anything deadlier. "I'm here on business."

Cortland's eyes flicked across to Liberty, who was still admiring the cap badge, and then back to Hudson. "Is she with you?"

"Yes, she's with me," said Hudson, "so you can press your little button under the counter to lock the door now." Then he leant in a little closer, "But don't try anything stupid this time."

Cortland did as he was instructed. "Believe me, I have learnt my lesson in that respect," said the dealer, reaching under the counter. "Though I must admit to not being particularly happy to see you again."

The door lock clicked and the window tinted black, causing Liberty to become alert. She rushed over to the counter, grabbed Cortland's silk shirt collar, and yanked him towards her. "If that door isn't open in five seconds, I'm going to throw you through it," she snarled.

"It's okay, Liberty, it's just to make sure we're not interrupted," said Hudson, as Cortland squirmed and made a sort of whimpering sound, like a needy puppy.

Liberty released the black-market dealer and took a step back, her cheeks flushing pink. "Oh, sorry," she said, and then pointed behind her with her thumb. "I'll, erm, just go back to browsing then."

Cortland anxiously watched Liberty return to surveying the contents of the shelves, as if she were a hornet, buzzing around the store.

"Sorry about that," said Hudson, rummaging inside his jacket for the CPU shard. "After the last time, I thought it was a good idea to hire a bodyguard."

"A bodyguard?!" exclaimed Cortland, but then he lowered his voice, ducking behind Hudson so that his body shielded him from Liberty's view. "A bodyguard?" he repeated, this time muttering the words in hushed tones.

"Oh, yeah," said Hudson, enjoying winding up the crooked dealer. "She knows about fifty ways to kill someone, just with her bare hands." Then he leaned in closer, and whispered, "I've already seen five of them..." before rocking back again.

Cortland's pale complexion had now become almost ghostly. Meanwhile, Hudson had finally managed to grasp his finger and thumb around the high-grade CPU shard. He pulled it out of the hidden compartment In his jacket, before placing it on the counter.

"Here you go," said Hudson, tapping the CPU shard with his index finger. "Same arrangement as before, except this time I won't give you quite such a knock-down price."

Some of the color returned to Cortland's face as he picked up the shard and eyed it greedily. He reached under the counter and lifted a toaster-sized piece of equipment onto the surface. He then placed the CPU shard into a slot that seemed ready-made for the relic and switched it on.

Neither of them spoke for the next couple of minutes, as Cortland assessed the shard. He made an assortment of humming sounds as he did so, all of which irritated Hudson immensely. He then shut off the device and removed the CPU shard, placing it back on the counter. Hudson noticed that he left a finger in contact with its surface, as if he were afraid that Hudson might snatch the relic back. The peculiar dealer may have known his stuff when it came to alien components, but his poker face had not improved since the last time they'd met.

"I'll give you one hundred and fifty, as before," said Cortland with a shifty smile.

The fact he'd offered this amount so quickly told Hudson that it was clearly worth more. "Two hundred," he said, straight-faced.

Cortland recoiled, "Please, what do you take me for?" he replied, "One sixty, and that's being generous."

Just at that moment Liberty reappeared and dumped the CET communications unit on the counter. Then she fetched a bunch of other alien components that Hudson didn't recognize and placed them alongside it. "One sixty-five, plus this lot, and you have a deal," she said, fixing Cortland with a penetrating stare.

The dealer shot back, as if the hornet had just landed in front of him, and the smile was wiped from his lips.

"Oh, well, that is rather a lot of equipment..." Cortland began, but Liberty just maintained her menacing stare. "But, very well, you strike a hard bargain, young lady." Then he blurted out a high-pitched laugh that was as fake and forced as his smile had been.

"Great, it's a deal then," said Hudson, pulling a credit scanner out of his jacket pocket, before resting it on the table. "I was starting to worry that I might have needed Liberty here to conduct some more aggressive negotiations, if you know what I mean..." Cortland's face drained of blood again; Hudson let him stew for a couple of seconds longer, before clasping a hand on his shoulder and shaking the dealer vigorously. "I'm kidding, I'm kidding!" he said, and then they all started laughing, creating a cacophony of fake mirth.

"Yes, well, I believe this concludes our business," said Cortland, hurriedly completing the credit transfer and handing the scanner back to Hudson. "Now, if you wouldn't mind, I am very busy."

Hudson placed the credit scanner back into his pocket, while Liberty packed the other alien components into her rucksack. She then looked at the bulky communications unit, met Hudson's eyes, and smiled innocently. Hudson shook his head and tutted, before picking up the bulky unit. It was far heavier than it looked.

"What is all this crap for, anyway?" complained Hudson, as he struggled to manipulate the bulky communications unit into a comfortable hold.

"It's not crap," said Liberty, huffily, but then added, "and you'll see soon enough..."

Cortland pressed the button under the counter to unlock the door, and Hudson staggered towards it, lugging the bulky piece of equipment under his arm.

"A pleasure doing business with you... again," said Hudson, shooting a smile back to Cortland, though he didn't appear to share the sentiment. Hudson was half-way out of the door, when he noticed Liberty wasn't with him. He turned around and saw that she had rushed back to one of the shelves, and picked up the brass-colored RAF badge. *I knew it...* Hudson told himself, feeling smug.

"Would you mind throwing this in too?" said Liberty, holding it up for Cortland to see.

The dealer squinted at the object, but then shrugged, "Yes, if you wish," he said. Though Hudson knew what he was actually saying was, 'Yes, if it will make you go away.'

Liberty beamed back at him and then shoved the badge into her jacket pocket, before joining Hudson at the door.

"See you next time, Mr. shady black-market dealer," chirped Liberty, before heading outside.

Cortland waved sarcastically and returned yet another artificial smile. Then he said, barely loud enough for Liberty to hear, "I most sincerely hope not."

CHAPTER 17

Swinsler folded his arms and lifted his chin defiantly, as he stood in front of the VCX-110 Light Courier Runner. It was like he was guarding it, the same way a doorman might block the entrance to a nightclub.

"Three-fifty is my final offer, take it or leave it," Swinsler said, repeating the proposition he'd made several times previously. "And even at that price, it is daylight robbery!"

Liberty had already stormed away, and was pacing up and down the forecourt, like a football coach whose team was being humiliated. Hudson was similarly furious, but was managing to keep a lid on his emotions, at least for the moment.

"Three hundred is what we agreed when I put the damn deposit down!" Hudson snarled back. "A deal's a deal, Swinsler."

"That was before you took my engineer off on your little adventures!" Swinsler hit back. "My costs have rocketed because of that, and these are costs I have to pass on to my customers." Then he jabbed an accusatory finger at Hudson. "This is your own fault, Mr. Powell."

Hudson looked around to see where Liberty had got to, fearful that she might do something rash, like set fire to the entire shipyard. Then he spotted her inspecting a row of ships near the entrance, all of which were pre-sold.

"Mr. Powell, are you listening?" said Swinsler. "Do we have a deal or not?"

Hudson sighed and rubbed the back of his neck. He was getting a little weary of the rollercoaster ride of fortunes he was experiencing. From having nothing, he'd hit the high of his first relic hunt with Liberty, to the low of nearly being killed by Cutler. Then back to a high of finding a great score, and rock bottom again when Griff had stolen it from him. It seemed that every step forward was met with two steps back. It was like being on a moving walkway that was always travelling in the opposite direction.

"Look, Swinsler, I don't have three-fifty," said Hudson, drawing on all his prior bartering experience to somehow make a deal. "With fuel and transit licenses, the most I can do is three, maybe three-five at an absolute push. That's still a great deal for you, especially for a ship that's not even space-worthy yet."

Swinsler's folded arms hugged his body even more tightly, and he shook his head angrily. "The price is three-fifty. Take it or leave it."

Hudson closed his eyes and drew in a deep breath of the sea air around Hunter's Point. He'd dealt with some obstinate salespeople, but usually there was a route through to an agreement. However, in the case of Swinsler, it was personal. As the ship dealer saw it, Hudson had stolen his employee, and Swinsler wanted to punish him for it. This wasn't about doing business, it was about petty point scoring.

Hudson heard the sound of boots scrunching the dirt of the forecourt underfoot, and opened his eyes to see Liberty approaching. She appeared calmer, but still wired, as if she was about to step into the ring and box Swinsler.

"Hey, Swinsler, does the new owner of that GE-909 know you stripped in engines from the 809 instead?"

Swinsler frowned, "What? What are you talking about?"

Liberty's eyes widened, feigning surprise. "And the Apogee seven-seven... I guess you mentioned that it has an astronics suite ripped from a ship twice its age?"

"Well, I mean, no, but..." Swinsler stammered. He had unfolded his arms and was looking flustered.

"But I'm sure you would have explained to the buyers of that Eclipse KA-420 that it was restored from a write-off?" Liberty continued. "Because if not, I guess that might affect its value, wouldn't you say?"

Hudson smiled; he'd forgotten that pretty much every ship in the yard had been pieced back together by Liberty. And now she was threatening to hit Swinsler where it hurt the most – his credit scanner.

"But... but this is blackmail!" Swinsler protested. "Extortion!"

Hudson shook his head, "No, this is business. Two-ninety is the price, or I guess we go knocking on a few people's doors..."

If Swinsler's face had gone any redder, it would have looked like a cranberry. However, Hudson knew that Liberty's threat had backed him into a corner. A few seconds later, the dealer relented. Hudson was glad, because any longer and he worried that the man's face would explode like a squashed grape. "Fine, two-ninety," he muttered, grabbing the credit scanner from Hudson to complete the transaction. "And good riddance to it." Then he jabbed his stubby finger at Liberty, "She could never make it fly anyway!"

Hudson was dying to let Swinsler in on the secret. Only he knew that Liberty had deceived Swinsler into believing the VCX-110 was in far worse condition than it actually was. He bit his tongue, however; the slimy ship salesman would find out soon enough. Glancing at Liberty out of the corner of his eye, he saw the same knowing look on her face.

Swinsler removed the registration fob from his belt and fiddled with it for a few seconds, before holding it out to Hudson. "Here, this will transfer the registry ID to you."

"It needs to be joint ownership," said Hudson, taking the fob and looking at Liberty. "This ship has two captains." Liberty smiled and then held the other end of the fob.

"Fine, I really don't care," said Swinsler, pressing his thumb to the device so that all three were now in contact with it. The fob registered their thumb prints and then ran retinal scans on each of them, before bleeping softly three times. Hudson and Liberty checked the display, which read, 'VCX-110, identification M7070. Registered owners: Powell, Hudson L. Devan, Liberty K. Please input registered callsign.'

"Registered callsign?" said Liberty, frowning at the display. "What's that?"

"It's a unique, custom identifier, though it's optional, so we don't have to enter anything," said

Hudson. He was about to clear the screen, when Liberty grabbed his hand.

"No, wait..." she said, and then looked up at the VCX-110. "Orion. She's called, Orion."

Hudson smiled, "You got it, Liberty." Then he held up the registration fob and said, "Designate callsign, Orion." The fob updated and blinked green, before deactivating.

"You have twenty-four hours to get it off my forecourt, or I'll charge you a storage fee," said Swinsler, snippily. Then his red face adopted a saccharin smile. "And since it doesn't fly, I expect to recoup my losses swiftly." Then he lifted his head and looked down his nose at both of them. "Now, if you don't mind, I have more important matters to attend to," Swinsler announced, before marching off back towards his pre-fab office block.

Hudson tossed the fob to Liberty who caught it and clipped it to her belt. He noticed that she had fashioned the RAF cap badge she'd acquired from Cortland's store into a belt buckle. "I wish I could be here to see his face," Hudson said, smiling. "Does that thing have enough juice in it to get us to Ride Spaceport for refueling?"

"That thing is called, 'Orion'," Liberty corrected him. "And, it's not supposed to, but I always made sure it had a few credits in the tank."

Hudson nodded and looked up at the ship. It really was a beauty. "Okay then, why don't you get the Orion fired up; I think it's high time we took this bird for a test flight."

Liberty looked like a kid at Christmas, and if he was honest, Hudson felt exactly the same way. He didn't know how long the rollercoaster would remain on this new peak, but he was going to enjoy it while it lasted.

Liberty ran ahead, climbing the ramp and entering the engineering section, while Hudson headed to the cockpit and strapped himself in. A few minutes later, the twin engines sparked into life, building to a rich, resonant purr. Hudson smiled as the instruments in the cockpit flickered into life. The status readouts showed that the flight systems were all green. Liberty hadn't been kidding about hiding the ship's true condition from Swinsler. Hudson grabbed the control column and began to prepare the ship for takeoff. Liberty appeared a few seconds later and slid into the second seat.

"We're all set, skipper," she said, pulling on her harness.

Hudson looked out of the cockpit glass and saw Swinsler standing in the middle of the forecourt, his hands on his head. He looked like someone who'd just crashed a brand-new car. Hudson knew it was cruel to take pleasure from the moment. Yet, at the same time, it was nice to see a swindler get ripped off for a change, instead of himself.

"Are you ready?" he said, glancing across to Liberty.

Liberty's eyes shone like supernovas, "Punch it, skipper!"

Hudson engaged the vertical lift thrusters, and the Orion rose majestically into the air above Hunter's Point, blowing Swinsler onto his backside in the process. Then he placed his hand on the main thruster control and pushed it forward, powering the ship higher and faster, and into the skyway lane towards Ride Spaceport. Liberty whooped and laughed, hammering her hands down on the arms of her chair, as they blasted across the Californian landscape.

"We did it, Hudson!" cried Liberty, "We can go anywhere we want!"

"Then you'd better think of a destination," said Hudson, smiling back at her. In fact, he hadn't stopped smiling since setting foot inside the Orion, and his face now ached from the strain. However, he didn't care. The Orion had lifted them both, and not just in terms of altitude. They were now free. He didn't care where they went next, because it didn't matter. All he knew in that moment was that he'd never felt more alive.

CHAPTER 18

With the credits they had left over after buying the Orion, Hudson had been able to take on fuel and supplies at Ride Spaceport. They even still had some money left in the bank. Then, like kids with new bikes, they couldn't wait to get out and see what the Orion could do. Their next hunt could wait a while, Hudson decided. This was a time to just enjoy their newfound independence.

For the first few hours after departing from Ride Spaceport and reaching orbit, Hudson had given the Orion a thorough shakedown. He tested all the systems, and pushed the maneuverable ship to its limits, and it hadn't missed a beat. Clearly, Liberty's restoration work had been executed with more than just professionalism. She had poured her heart and soul into the ship too. Even so, all throughout the shakedown tests, Liberty had flitted between the cockpit and the engineering section in order to make further refinements and modifications. Her efforts had paid off, fine-tuning the ship's already impeccable performance even more acutely. And when the time had come to throttle back and sit down for a well-earned meal, Hudson had freely admitted that it was the best ship he'd ever flown. Hands down. No questions.

Sharing a meal together in the living space of the Orion had made Hudson realize something else too. Nothing about the ship felt unfamiliar to him. The VCX-110 Light Courier Runner was roomy enough to accommodate three crew cabins, and with only the two of them on-board, it felt spacious and comfortable. But it was more than just comfort that Hudson felt; it was an instinctive sense of belonging. It felt like he'd lived on the ship for a decade already. It was, as Liberty had already commented to him, a feeling of being home.

Home... thought Hudson. *I've never really had a home...* He'd lived in many places during his life, but none had felt special to him. Home was a concept that was going to take some getting used to, he realized. But Liberty was right, the Orion wasn't just a ship, and it wasn't merely a vessel that unlocked access to the galaxy. It was almost like another member of the crew.

"So, where shall we head to first?" wondered Hudson, relaxing back on the semi-circular couch and placing his beer down on the table.

Liberty had the CET communications unit in front of her and was working on it. The other alien components she'd bartered from the Antiques and Curiosity Shoppe were scattered alongside it. "I don't know," she murmured, shoving an alien component into the communications unit and soldering it in place. "I guess we just see where the wind blows us. Though, I've always wanted to see Mars."

"It's been a while since I've been in MP territory," replied Hudson. "There are certainly some good portal worlds out there. The Martians can be a little uptight, though." Then Hudson leant in to get a closer look at the contraption Liberty was modifying. "What are you up to, anyway, Dr. Frankenstein? Other than making a damned mess, that is."

Liberty scowled at him over the top of the communications unit, "I'm experimenting..." she answered, mysteriously.

"With what? The best way to make a mess on our new ship?" said Hudson. He knew Liberty was being deliberately obtuse, in response to his snarky comment about her tidiness, or lack thereof.

"If you must know, I'm working on an idea to hook in that crystal to the ship's communications and sensor array," said Liberty. She then again ducked behind the old CET communications unit so that Hudson could only see the top of her head. "If it is a key part of some alien communication device, I might be able to make an interface using a blend of our tech and alien components."

"To what end?" asked Hudson, becoming more interested now that Liberty had mentioned the crystal. "I mean, what do you think it will do?

Smoke from the soldering iron puffed up above the device, making it look like Liberty's hair was on fire. Then she reappeared, blew a strand of loose hair away from her face and put down the iron. "I don't know – like I said, I'm experimenting. Crystals and crystalline materials have been used in everything from early radio systems to semiconductors." Then she pointed to Hudson's jacket. "Our little crystal is something entirely new though, so who knows what it's capable of." Then she patted the modified communications unit like a dog, and added, "I'm hoping that this little Frankenstein contraption might help us discover what it can actually do."

Hudson downed the remaining contents of his beer and then removed the crystal from his jacket pocket. He slid it over to Liberty and then relaxed back again. "Just try not to blow us up, okay?"

"I'll do my best," replied Liberty, sarcastically. She then picked up the crystal and placed it inside the device, before closing up the rear panel.

The computer console on the wall behind Hudson's head bleeped an alert, and he twisted around to check it. "That's odd, there's a ship approaching," he said, scowling at the readout.

Liberty shuffled around the semi-circular couch so that she could also read the screen. "Could it just be a regular CET patrol?"

Hudson could feel the hairs on the back of his neck standing on end. Something felt off. "I don't know, but I think we should get to the cockpit."

Liberty nodded and slid back around the couch, grabbing the modified device and placing it in a storage compartment underneath the table. She then hurried after Hudson, who was already jogging along the central walkway and up the shallow flight of stairs to the cockpit.

Hudson was already strapped into his seat when Liberty arrived, hurriedly activating the ship's engine and thruster controls.

"You'd better buckle up," said Hudson, grabbing the control column and pushing the throttle forward. "Take a look at the classification of the ship that's heading for us."

Liberty barely had time to pull the harness tight before the two-g burn pressed her back into her seat. She fought back against the force of the acceleration and checked her console. "FS-31 Patrol Craft, Hawk-1333F," she read aloud, and then the penny dropped. "Oh, you have got to be kidding me! That's Cutler's ship!"

CHAPTER 19

Hudson wasted no time in breaking orbit, before entering the co-ordinates for one of the near-Earth portals into the nav computer. "He's a persistent little bastard, I'll give him that," he said, fighting with the controls to keep them on course.

Liberty frowned as the new navigation plan flashed up on her console screen. "Brahms Three? I thought we were heading to Mars?"

"Mars will have to wait, I'm afraid," said Hudson, watching the target blip on his panel. Cutler's ship was still some distance away, but the FS-31 class was fast, and Cutler was likely used to high-g travel. "It will take days to reach Mars, and Cutler will be on top of us long before then."

"So why not just head back to Earth?" asked Liberty, "Surely, he can't catch up with us, before we make re-entry?"

Hudson locked in their trajectory and rested his head back into the seat, releasing some of the extra tension in his neck. He glanced over to Liberty, and saw she was looking increasingly more concerned. Though Hudson reasoned that her pained expression could also have been due to the extra forces acting on her body.

"We could go back to Earth, but then we're back at square one," said Hudson. "We take off again, and he comes after us again. Earth just isn't safe."

"And Brahms Three is?" exclaimed Liberty.

Though it was framed as a question, Hudson could tell it wasn't intended as one. After the stories he'd told her, on top of her already basement-level opinion of the world, Hudson knew that 'safe' was not a word that Liberty would ascribe to Brahms Three.

"Besides, I thought you hated that planet," Liberty added, after Hudson remained silent.

"We're not going there to sight-see," said Hudson, watching the range indicator closely, and noting that Cutler was gaining on them. "We need a safe harbor, and I know someone on Brahms Three who might help us out."

Liberty sighed and relaxed, letting the chair take the strain. "Whatever you say, skipper..." But then she tilted her head across to him again, "I don't see why it matters if he catches up with us, anyway. What's the worst he can do? Flip the bird at us through the cockpit window?"

Hudson pushed the engines harder, accelerating at two-point-five g. That would keep them out of reach of Cutler for the time being, but he knew he'd still need to rotate the engines and decelerate hard before he could make the portal transition. And that would give Cutler the window of opportunity he needed.

"I'm afraid his plan is to launch more than just insults at us," said Hudson, glancing over to Liberty. "He means to shoot us down."

"What?" Liberty would have sprung out of her seat had it not been for the harness and the additional force pressing down on her. "But private vessels aren't allowed to carry weapons in CET space; it's against the law."

Hudson remembered back to his engagement with the relic hunter smuggler on Vivaldi One. He'd made the same assumption then that Liberty had just made, and it had almost got him blown away.

"Trust me, I've learnt the hard way that these people don't obey the law," he said, glancing down to the range indicator again. He estimated that Cutler would get maybe sixty seconds before he was within the perimeter of the portal checkpoint. "But, if we're lucky, there will be a CET patrol craft on-station at the portal checkpoint. So long as we can get inside the checkpoint perimeter, Cutler will have to break off, or otherwise risk an all-out engagement with the CET military."

"That sounds like a whole lot of assumptions, skipper," said Liberty.

"I know, but here's another... Our successful escape also assumes we can pass through the portal, before being blown to pieces."

"I already don't like this plan," interrupted Liberty, but Hudson ignored her, and continued.

"Once we're through, we'll be able to get a head-start on them on the other side, even if they do follow us."

"How?" asked Liberty. "Surely, they'll just land right on top of us again?"

Hudson smiled at Liberty, "This is where I'm counting on the advantage of a genius engineer co-captain..."

Liberty rolled her eyes, "Did I already mention that I hate this idea?"

"Portal transitions knock out the main drive systems," Hudson went on, bursting through Liberty's bubble of sarcasm like a dart. "A good crew can restart them and be underway again in maybe fifteen minutes. But I'm betting you can crank our engines a lot faster. That will give us the lead we need to make the second transition to Brahms Three."

"I hope you're right," said Liberty, gripping the arms of the chair.

"We'll find out soon enough," said Hudson, throttling back and then rotating the engine pods one hundred and eighty degrees. "Flip your seat," he called out to Liberty, showing her the location of the lever. "We're going to decelerate hard and then make our run for the portal checkpoint."

Liberty nodded and switched her seat to face the rear of the cockpit. As soon as it had locked into place, the acceleration slammed her back into her seat again. "I hate high-g travel!" she called out, over the roar of the engines.

Hudson steeled himself against the forces acting on his body, but just managed to call out, "You'll hate getting shot at more." Either Liberty didn't find the joke amusing, or she was in too much pain to answer.

Besides the rattle of deck plates and the thrum of their engines, neither spoke for the next couple of minutes. Hudson's eyes didn't leave the range indicators on the consoles that had swung around with his chair. He was constantly comparing their distance to the checkpoint portal to Cutler's ever-decreasing range to them. *Shit, this is going to be close...* he thought, but he kept that to himself, for fear of stressing out Liberty more than was necessary. He had only casually described her upcoming role in their escape, but he was banking on Liberty's skill more than she realized. The truth was that if they couldn't start their engines fast, they'd be a sitting duck for whatever illicit weaponry Cutler's ship had in store for them. "Get ready to flip your chair back in three... two... one... now!"

Hudson and Liberty rotated their seats back to face the main cockpit instruments again. The portal checkpoint rapidly swung into view directly ahead. Far from simple toll-booths in space, most checkpoints were akin to elaborate highway rest stops, containing space stations and refueling facilities. Hudson could see that seven other ships were already waiting in line to transit, but he hadn't yet picked up a CET patrol.

He checked the scanners and saw that Cutler's ship was only seconds behind them. "Shit, he must have decelerated harder than us," said Hudson, setting a direct course for the rest stop station. "Hold on, this might get a little hairy..."

The proximity alert sounded, and Hudson thrust the Orion hard to port, as tracer rounds snaked out ahead of them. Then the alert sounded again as the space station started to engulf the cockpit glass.

The radio automatically switched on to the alert frequency, and an urgent broadcast from the space station came through the speaker. "VCX-110, M7070-Orion, abort approach immediately or you will be fired upon."

"Hudson..." Liberty called out, gripping the arms of her seat so tightly that the blood drained from her knuckles.

Hudson pulsed the thrusters again, pushing the Orion down below the station's belly. Another volley of tracer fire rushed past the window, and an alarm sounded on Liberty's console. "Outer hull breach in the cargo hold!" she called out, checking the damage readout. "It hasn't penetrated though; we're okay."

Hudson swung the ship up, trying to hug the space station as closely as possible. Another warning broadcast filled the cabin, and Hudson knew he'd have to break off soon, otherwise the station would start shooting at them too. Then he spotted a CET transponder on the navigation scanner and breathed a sigh of relief.

"Liberty, radio that CET patrol ship," Hudson called over to the second seat, while continuing to weave a chaotic course. "Tell them we're under attack."

Liberty nodded and then grabbed her headset, before switching to the indicated channel. "CET Patrol Craft, this is VCX-110, M7070-Orion. We are under attack by bandits! FS-31 Patrol Craft Hawk-1333F has opened fire. Please respond!"

Hudson and Liberty waited anxiously until the response crackled through the speakers. "Message acknowledged. Stand by, Orion..."

Hudson checked the navigation scanner and saw the patrol craft start to accelerate towards their position. "Good work, Liberty, it looks like they're coming to the rescue," he said, veering away from the station and heading towards the portal gate. Then he smiled over at her. "Bandits, though? This isn't the Wild West!"

Liberty laughed, "You could have fooled me..."

Just then the CET patrol craft shot above them and Hudson saw it fire a burst from its cannons.

"Did they shoot him down?" asked Liberty, hopefully.

Hudson could still see Cutler's ship on the navigation scanner, and shook his head. "No, it was likely just a warning shot across their bow," he said, but then noticed that the ship had veered away. "Cutler has broken off; now's our chance to make a run for the portal."

Hudson powered up the main engines and angled the nose of the Orion straight for the front of the line.

"Isn't there a queue for a reason?" asked Liberty. Her facial muscles had already cycled through about a dozen different ways to express fear, concern and anxiety, but Hudson was impressed that she still managed to discover a new one.

"Queues are for losers and British people," said Hudson, dismissively. A message flashed up on their screens from the gate controller. "VCX-110, M7070-Orion – you are not cleared for transit. All line jumpers will be subject to a 5000-credit fine."

"Sounds like queues are for people who don't want to bankrupt themselves..." added Liberty, with a healthy slice of snark.

Hudson continued to power towards the portal. He knew about the fines, and he also knew there was a risk they'd emerge on the other side of the portal directly into the path of a freighter. Like a yacht sailing in front of an oil tanker, this was something that could spoil a pilot's day pretty quickly. But neither of these prospects were worse than the alternative.

"We could be sitting in that queue for an hour," said Hudson, calmly. "That's an hour where Cutler can devise any number of creative methods of cracking open our hull like an egg." He turned to face her. "So, what's it to be? Five thousand credits, or a cold, miserable death in space?"

Liberty shook her head and growled her acceptance. "Fine, run the portal," she said folding her arms. "But I'm going to get that five-grand back from Cutler Wendell one day, even if I have to beat it out of him."

CHAPTER 20

Despite Liberty's objections, and Hudson's own reservations concerning the risks of running a portal, the plan had actually worked. Not only had they helpfully not emerged into the path of an oncoming ship, but Liberty had re-started the engines in four minutes flat. The first was sheer, dumb luck, while the second was skill, combined with an intrinsic knowledge of what made the Orion tick.

After a quick fly-by of Chopin Four, they had transited though the portal to Brahms Three in less than an hour. This was in part due to another uncomfortable two-point-five-g burn, and the fact that no-one else appeared desperate enough to want to travel to Brahms Three. In that time, there had been no further sign of Cutler's ship. With any luck, they had been arrested by the CET, Hudson hoped. However, knowing Cutler Wendell, he assumed the mercenary had probably slimed or bribed his way out of trouble again. Either way, he knew it wouldn't be the last he saw of him.

Hudson touched down the Orion in the small spaceport on the edge of Brahms Three's scavenger town, and powered down. His body ached from the force of their prolonged acceleration. However, even without the added g-forces, the ordeal of their escape had caused his muscles to remain tense.

"I don't know about you, but I need a drink," said Hudson. He unclipped his harness and then stretched his arms and legs, like a cat that had just woken from a long nap.

Liberty got up too and straightened out the kinks in her neck, "I think we just blew all your drinking money getting away from Cutler."

Hudson quickly checked the credit scanner, noting that the CET had already automatically deducted the fine for running the portal. *Typical bureaucrats...* he thought. *Useless at pretty much everything, apart from collecting money.* "We still have enough for the docking fee and to top up our fuel," Hudson said, sliding the scanner back into his pocket. "But after that, we are going to need to bag another score."

Hudson headed out of the cockpit, beckoning Liberty to follow him. "Anyway, the bar I have in mind doesn't accept credits." He stopped and smiled back at her, "And I know you're still hiding away some hardbucks inside that snazzy getup of yours."

"If by 'snazzy getup' you mean my clothes, then I don't know what you're talking about," Liberty answered, haughtily.

"Come on, don't hold out on me," replied Hudson, stepping down the short flight of stairs to the main deck. "Besides, there's someone I want to introduce you to."

Liberty shook her head and followed, "Looking at the state of this town, I shudder to think who..."

Hudson took care of the landing fee, while Liberty refueled the ship. Considering the relative sportiness of their recent maneuvers, it hadn't used nearly as much fuel as Hudson had expected. Liberty put this down to a number of personal modifications to the fueling system and engines that had improved efficiency. Hudson just nodded and smiled as she detailed the various changes, not understanding a word of it.

Once they were done, Hudson led Liberty out of the space port and into the stifling heat of the scavenger town. As usual, the streets were filled with the reverberant, deep bass thud of the nightclubs, and the musky scent of street food, sweat and incense.

"You take me to all the nicest places," said Liberty. She was frowning at the streets, lined on either side by converted shipping containers stacked two or three high. As she was taking in the new setting, a man in a long black coat that seemed entirely inappropriate for the stuffy climate sauntered up to her. He slid a sweaty, grime-smudged hand out of the coat and held up a clear bag, containing a leafy, yellow substance.

"Hey, darlin', looking to buy some..."

"Walk away now, or I break all your fingers..." Liberty interrupted, before the man could finish his sentence. The man peered back into her eyes, glanced across to Hudson, who merely shrugged, and then quickly withdrew his hand and hurried away.

"See, you're a hit with the locals already," said Hudson, cheerfully.

"Someone's getting hit, that's for sure," said Liberty, coolly.

Hudson laughed; Liberty's mastery of passive aggression never ceased to amaze him. "Come on, the place we're headed to is just a couple of streets along from here."

They continued on, playing a game of counting the number of different types of proposition that each received en route. Liberty reached seven by the time they arrived at the door to the Landing Strip, compared to five for Hudson. However, Hudson still declared himself the winner. This was based on the fact that two shady underworld types had actually offered to buy Liberty from him, and he had selflessly refused. Liberty disputed this claim, saying that the old crone who'd asked, 'how much for an hour with your dad?' trumped them all. In the end, they called it a draw, and pushed through the door into the bar.

"Hudson Powell!" bellowed Ma, as Hudson's boots clomped across the wooden floor of the Landing Strip. "Well shit – you're not dead!"

"Not yet..." said Hudson, who was then pulled into a tight bear-hug by the wiry older woman. Hudson could feel his feet lifting off the floor as Ma continued to squeeze the air from his lungs. He thought he might pass out, before she eventually released her hold on him. His feet thudded to the floor, as if he was an empty beer barrel that Ma had just changed.

"This calls for a celebration!" Ma declared, slapping her hand on the bar. This had the effect of waking up a white-haired old man at the far end of the counter, who had apparently passed out. He, along with five others sitting at various tables, were the only others in the bar.

Ma ducked down under the counter and returned moments later with a square whiskey bottle and two tumblers. She was half-way through pouring the first measure when she noticed Liberty. She was still standing mid-way between the door and the counter. Liberty had the look of someone who'd walked into a party and suddenly realized she didn't know a soul there.

"Who's the girl?" Ma whispered to Hudson, while pouring the second measure.

Hudson twisted back and ushered Liberty forward. "Martina Nunes, meet Liberty Devan." Then he turned back to Ma and smiled, "Co-captain of the good ship, Orion."

"You got a ship?" said Ma, beaming first at Hudson and then at Liberty. Hudson nodded. "And you got a crew?" Hudson nodded again. "And you two are relic hunters?" Hudson laughed, and nodded for a third time. Ma suddenly let out an excited shriek that almost knocked Hudson off his stool. Then the former relic hunter reached over and grabbed Liberty, pulling her into a hug and practically smothering her face against her bosom. She then dropped Liberty and reached under the counter for another tumbler, before slamming it down on the counter with gusto.

"So, how did you two meet?" asked Ma, filling Liberty's tumbler from the anonymous, square bottle. "I'll bet it was saving his ass from another one of his dumb schemes."

"Hey!" protested Hudson, but Ma just shushed him.

"I warned him off buying the crappy ships on sale at the yard I worked at," said Liberty, picking up the tumbler, "but then I decided he was a sort of okay-ish kinda guy, and decided to allow him the honor of being my pilot."

Ma laughed and raised an eyebrow at Hudson, who was scowling.

"That's not exactly how it went down," sighed Hudson, "but I guess it's close enough."

"Some kind of bad-ass you got here," said Ma, nudging Hudson's arm. "And about time too. You've been kicking your sorry ass around this galaxy on your own for too long." Then she picked up her tumbler, waited for Hudson to raise his, and proposed a toast. "To the hunt."

Hudson and Liberty repeated the toast and then they all drained the contents of the tumblers. Hudson had almost forgotten just how potent Ma's distillation was. It stole the breath from him, like Ma's hug. He glanced across to Liberty, who had one eye shut, the other twitching involuntarily. She was slapping her hand on the bar as if tapping out to an MMA submission hold.

"Shit, Ma, are you making this stuff stronger with each batch?" said Hudson, after he was finally able to speak.

"Yeah, this one has a nice, smooth kick to it," she said, as if describing a bottle of mild hot sauce. Then she re-filled all the tumblers and looked at Hudson intently. "So, what really brings you back to Brahms Three? I'm sure as hell it's not the scenery."

Hudson took a sip of the whiskey and became more solemn. "To tell you the truth, we need your help," he began. This time, Ma didn't respond with a jibe or witty quip. She just held Hudson's eyes and listened attentively, while Hudson detailed their adventures so far.

Several minutes and another two whiskeys later, Hudson had finished, and Ma rocked back on her heels, looking deep in thought.

"And you say this Logan Griff and Cutler Wendell won't stop coming after you?" Ma asked. Hudson shook his head. Ma again thought for a moment, before saying, "Okay, Hudson, I'll do you a deal. I'll act as a bank for any relics and hardbucks you want to put in safe storage. And I'll make sure that your ship," she hesitated and glanced at Liberty, "what was its name again?"

"The Orion," said Liberty, smiling.

"I'll make sure no-one messes with the Orion, while it's docked at Brahms Three," Ma continued. "And, this place will always be a sanctuary, should you need it. In here, I don't care whether you're a hunter, an RGF cop or a CET soldier. This is my place, and it's my rules. In here, you're safe." Then she looked over at Liberty again. "Both of you."

Hudson blew out a relaxed breath, "Thanks, Ma, I knew I could count on you."

"Don't thank me yet," said Ma, keenly, "It'll cost you ten per cent of whatever you stash here." Then she tapped the bottle. "And you're going to have to start paying for all the damn whiskey you're drinking too."

Ma's mention of payment seemed to jolt Liberty into action. She lowered the zip on her jacket and then reached inside, before pulling out a small stack of hard bucks.

"See, I knew you were holding out on me!" said Hudson, slapping his hand on the counter, triumphantly.

Liberty offered the hardbucks to Ma, but she just waved them off. "This is a celebration, and it's on me," said Ma, "so, shove them back where you found them."

"Thanks, Martina," said Liberty, tucking the notes away again.

The former hunter smiled, "Call me Ma."

Just then the door swung open and heavy boots thudded inside. Hudson could see Ma's eyes sharpen, like a hawk that had spotted a potential prey.

The door closed again, and Hudson heard one set of boots walking up behind him. A stool screeched across the wooden floor as it was drawn back from under the counter top, and a woman sat down. Hudson looked over, noting the body-hugging, but rugged-looking pants, and the fitted jacket that reflected the strip lights in the bar like Samurai armor. He didn't need to look up at the woman's face to know who it was.

"Whiskey," said Tory Bellona, looking at Ma, before twisting on her stool to face Hudson.

CHAPTER 21

Hudson knew that Tory's arrival meant that Cutler Wendell wouldn't be far behind. He glanced up at Ma, indicating the danger with a simple raising of his eyebrows. Ma acknowledged the gesture with an almost imperceptible nod of her head, and then walked over in front of Tory. Peering into the mercenary's cold blue eyes, she placed an old, chipped tumbler on the counter top, grabbed a bottle of her cheapest whiskey, and filled the glass.

Hudson glanced over at Liberty, noting that she had already shifted position, ready to spring into action if required. Then he slid off his stool and turned to see Cutler Wendell, standing just inside the door, as if waiting for an invitation.

"Fancy seeing you here," said Hudson, as Cutler stared back at him glassily.

"You know, I'm getting really tired of chasing you around the galaxy," said Cutler, taking a single step forward. It was hard to tell if he was being sarcastic or genuine, given the measured, almost sinister way in which he spoke every word.

"Then why don't you stop doing it, dumbass?" replied Hudson. He decided that his more macho, 'relic hunter' persona was merited, given the circumstances. Then he noticed that Cutler was armed, and that the strap on his holster had already been popped open, before he'd entered the bar. Hudson was still wearing the shoulder holster and pistol that Tory had given him, but it was still fastened in place. That, coupled with the numerous whiskeys he'd already knocked back, didn't give him much confidence of coming out on top in a quickdraw contest.

Hudson stole another glance over to Tory, who had downed the first shot. She was rudely tapping the chipped tumbler with her index finger, while staring at Ma. The last time Hudson had seen anyone look at Ma the way Tory was now, that person had ended up in the infirmary with a shattered nose. Hudson noticed that Tory was also armed with her signature single action revolver.

"Oh, I intend to stop, right here, on this shitty little world," Cutler continued, drawing Hudson's attention back to the mercenary. "Because I can shoot you right now, and be gone before the CET even realizes what happened."

Hudson could see Cutler's fingers twitching, like a Wild West gunslinger, and he felt his pulse quicken. Cutler wasn't bluffing, and he was also correct; he could shoot Hudson and be gone, before he would be able to react. And from what he'd seen of the CET forces on Brahms Three, it was also true that their response would likely be less than effective. He tried to think of a way out, but the truth was he was cornered.

Cutler's hand moved towards his weapon, but before his fingers reached the grip, Tory had drawn her revolver and slammed it down on the counter, finger on the trigger. Tory's action was like springing a trap. The instant her weapon had been drawn, chairs screeched and the sound of hands clasping metal echoed around the room. The six other occupants of the bar had woken from their apparent stupors, and all drawn weapons. Three barrels each were now levelled at Tory and Cutler. Even the white-haired old man, who had been passed out at the far end of the counter when Hudson arrived, had pulled a gun. He was aiming it at Tory with a steadier hand than Hudson could have managed in that moment.

Hudson remained motionless; still stuck for what to do next. But at least the immediate threat had gone. Tory's action had inadvertently reversed Cutler's advantage. Now, there was no chance of him shooting Hudson, without one of the six other weapons in the room filling Cutler with holes first.

Had that been Tory's plan all along? Hudson thought to himself, wondering if once again Tory Bellona had come to his aid. He looked at Tory's six-shooter, still resting on the counter with the mercenary's hand around the grip. But the hammer wasn't cocked. He met Tory's eyes and there was an immediate understanding between them.

Ma was the first person to make a move. She carefully prised the six-shooter from Tory's hand, and stuffed it down the waistband of her pants.

"I'll be wanting that back," said Tory, calmly, before she rocked back on her stool.

Ma's eyes sharpened, "That depends on whether you walk out of here, or get carried out on a stretcher." Then with the white-haired man still covering Tory, Ma stepped around the bar and made her way towards Cutler Wendell. Her old relic hunter boots, still polished to perfection, thudded on the solid wood floor with a percussive timbre like gunshots. Cutler glared back at her, but took no action as Ma reached down and removed the weapon from his holster. She released the magazine and then popped out the round in the chamber, before tossing the two parts of the weapon onto a table beside the door.

"I take it you're Cutler Wendell?" said Ma, looking at Cutler as if he'd just let out a fart.

"This is none of your concern, barkeep, so I suggest you back off," said Cutler, ignoring her question. "You have no idea who you're dealing with."

Ma smiled, "I've dealt with pissant little mercs like you since before you could tie your own shoelaces." Then without warning she snatched the ship registration fob from his belt. Cutler tried to grab it back, but Ma shoved him against the door, then snapped a jab into his face as he rebounded towards her. Cutler fought back, but Ma caught his wrist and twisted his arm into a lock, causing him to cry out in pain.

Tory practically flew off the seat towards Ma, but then six weapons instantly turned on her, forcing her to stop a couple of paces short of striking distance. Tory glared at each man and woman who had aimed a weapon at her, then turned back to Ma. The older woman met her eyes, while still ensuring Cutler was incapacitated in the painful restraining hold. Ma held up the registration fob, read the ship ID, and then tossed the fob to Tory, who caught it.

"Here's what's going to happen," said Ma, maneuvering Cutler between her and Tory. "You're going to leave Brahms Three within the next hour, and you're not going to come back."

"You don't tell me what to do, lady," said Tory. Hudson could see the fire in her eyes, burning with the same malevolence he'd seen on Vivaldi One and Bach Two. "I go where I please."

"Not in this town," said Ma, defiantly, while Cutler still squirmed at her feet. "If Hawk-1333F ever touches down on this planet again, I'll have it stripped for parts, before you've even set foot off the ramp."

"There are other ways to get here," said Tory, seeming not to care about the threat to the ship, "and there are other places to land."

"Yes, there are," replied Ma, throwing Cutler down in front of Tory. Cutler cradled his arm, his face contorted in pain. "But you're not welcome here. So if you do come back, know that you won't ever leave again. Not while I'm around."

Tory helped Cutler to his feet. He growled and spat blood on to the floor from the cut lip that Ma had given him earlier. He shook off Tory's hold on him, causing the female mercenary to look even more incensed than she already was, and then jabbed a finger at Hudson.

"You won't stay on this planet forever," he snarled. "It doesn't matter where you go, I'll be following. Sooner or later, your luck is going to run out, Hudson Powell."

Hudson got off the stool and strode up to Cutler. "Maybe you're right," he replied, "but today is not that day."

Ma opened the door, "One hour," she said, locking eyes with Cutler. "If you're not gone in one hour, it's open season on your ship, on you, and on your partner here too."

Cutler spat another glob of bloodied spittle onto the floor and then stormed out. Ma watched him closely until he was out in the street and then turned to Tory, "You too, lady."

Hudson stepped up to Tory and then plucked the six-shooter out of Ma's waistband. The former relic hunter eyed Hudson suspiciously, as he then offered the revolver back to Tory, grip first. Tory looked at Hudson, the fire in her eyes now reduced to burning embers, and took the weapon. She stroked her finger across Hudson's hand as she did so, before sliding it carefully back into her holster.

Tory then glanced over at Liberty, before pacing towards the door, as casually as if she were out on a morning stroll. She stopped on the threshold, and then reached into her armored jacket pocket. For a moment, Hudson held his breath, afraid of what Tory was going to do next. However, instead of pulling out one of her many other weapons, Tory held up a one hundred-dollar hardbuck note. She straightened it out and then offered it to Ma.

"Thanks for the drink," she said, coolly. Ma took the note, nodding respectfully. Then they all watched as Tory moved outside, without another word or a second look back.

Ma pocketed the money and then shut the door behind her. Almost immediately the patrons of the bar put their weapons away, and continued drinking and chatting as if nothing had happened.

It was so surreal that Hudson actually laughed out loud.

"Does this sort of thing happen often?" he asked, still amazed by the synchronized response of the others in the room.

Ma smiled, "More often than you'd think." She then walked back behind the bar, popped the caps off six beers, and slid them along to the white-haired old man at the end of the counter. He caught them all, distributed five to the other patrons in the room, before sitting back down at the bar. He raised his bottle to Ma and then Hudson and Liberty, before taking a healthy swig. Ma refilled the whiskey tumblers, and then Hudson sat back down at the counter too.

"Who was the woman?" Ma asked, taking a sip of her drink.

"You mean Psycho Lady?" said Liberty, pulling her stool closer to Hudson's. "You've heard of a love-hate relationship? Well these two have more of a love-murder relationship."

Hudson rolled his eyes, "Tory isn't all bad," he said, rubbing the back of his hand where Tory's finger had stroked it. "I just haven't worked out which part of her is good yet, that's all." Then he looked at Liberty and raised a wagging finger at her, realizing he'd just opened himself up to innuendo. "And don't say it, don't you dare!"

Liberty smiled, "I don't need to say anything; it's written all over your face like one of the neon signs out in the street."

They all laughed, which helped to relieve some of the pent-up tension. Then Ma shrugged and added, "Well, if you ask me that lady probably just saved your lives."

Liberty folded her arms, "How do you work that one out? She was the first to pull a gun. Seems like a funny way to save someone."

"Oh, I don't disagree," Ma replied, "but that weapon was an old Colt Frontier Six-Shooter. In order to fire one of those, you have to manually pull back the hammer, and her weapon wasn't cocked."

Liberty now shrugged, "Maybe she just made a mistake and forgot to do it?"

Ma shook her head confidently, "I've known mercenaries like her before. Whatever else she might be, she's a pro. And pros don't make that sort of mistake. She never had any intention of shooting, but she also made sure you didn't get shot."

Hudson nodded and drank the whiskey. More than anything, he was just glad that Ma had picked up on Tory's subtle actions too. It meant that his hope about Tory being the person he wanted her to be wasn't just a concoction of his own mind. Still, so long as she remained with Cutler, Tory was still a threat.

Hudson sighed and then looked at Liberty, "I think it's about time we made a move."

"Are you sure?" asked Liberty, "We could just hunt on the wreck here at Brahms Three."

Hudson shook his head, "I won't let Cutler dictate where we go or what we do. We've a whole galaxy to explore, and I say we go out and explore it. Screw that guy." Then he held up his hands, apologetically, "With your approval, of course, co-captain Devan."

Liberty lifted the whiskey tumbler to her lips. "Do you really need to ask?" she replied, before necking the contents and slamming the glass back down on the counter.

CHAPTER 22

Despite their defiant attitude to Cutler's threats, Hudson and Liberty had kept a watchful eye on the dark street corners as they walked back to the ship. To Cutler, Hudson was no longer just a bounty; it had become personal. As such, he doubted Cutler would take him out by stealth; he'd want Hudson to know he'd got him. Still, he wasn't taking any chances, and by the time they'd reached the spaceport, it was clear that Hawk-1333F had already departed. Hudson knew they were safe, at least for now.

After they had blasted off from Brahms Three, Hudson had proposed heading back to the solar system and then on to Mars. Mars had been Liberty's preferred destination, prior to Cutler's attack, but she had mysteriously asked Hudson to wait. As such, for the last three hours, Hudson had been watching Brahms Three slowly rotate beneath him, as the Orion sat in a low orbit above the sweaty little planet. During this time, Liberty had been back in the living quarters. She was feverishly working on the device she was building to interface with the alien crystal. A spread of alien and Earth-based electronics were strewn all across the table and floor. The whole mess had made Hudson's teeth itch. This was why he'd retired to the calm and, more importantly, tidy surroundings of the cockpit. He felt like he was just about to nod off, when Liberty burst in through the door, holding the contraption in both hands.

"Sleeping on the job?" asked Liberty, bustling to the front of the cockpit and setting the device down in front of the instrument panel.

"If my job is sitting on my ass, waiting for you, then I'm guilty as charged," replied Hudson, yawning. Then he swung his seat towards Liberty, and peered down at the device. "Any luck with whatever that thing is?"

Liberty was already busy unscrewing a panel underneath the flight deck. "That's what I'm here to find out," she said, releasing the final screw and then pulling the panel away. She rested it and the four screws on her seat and then slid the hefty piece of equipment into the space. It seemed to slot in as if purpose-designed for the location.

"At this stage, I feel the need to reiterate my point about not blowing us up," said Hudson, as a series of lights and indicators on the contraption blinked chaotically. He could see the crystal through a clear window in the center, reflecting the cockpit lights in its uniquely alien way.

Liberty started to secure the device in place using the screws she'd removed earlier. "How about you do the flying and leave the engineering stuff to me?"

"It's the 'not being blown up' stuff I'm most interested in right now," replied Hudson, refusing to let it go, like a dog with a bone.

Liberty finished attaching the final screw and slid into her seat, tossing the unwanted metal panel onto the deck beside her. Hudson rolled his eyes, pushed himself out of the pilot's seat and picked up the panel. "It would be nice if you didn't leave the 'tidying up stuff' all to me too." He moved to the rear of the cockpit and put the unwanted panel into a storage compartment. Suddenly, the lights in the cockpit flickered, and an alarm rang out on Liberty's console.

"What is it?" Hudson asked, darting back to check the cause of the alarm. "Is it Cutler's ship?" he asked, frantically checking the navigation scanner. But other than a couple of ships heading for the portal that were clearly identified as freighters, the scanner was clear. Then he noticed something he'd not spotted before. Nearby portal coordinates were always visible on the navigation scanner. Ship's scanners were all tuned to detect the portal's unique Shaak radiation signature.

However, the navigation scanner on the Orion wasn't just picking up one portal – it was showing two.

"It's not Cutler's ship," said Liberty, answering Hudson's original question. She had been focused on her console screen, studying a raft of data that made little sense to Hudson. "To be honest, I'm not entirely sure what it is, but we're certainly picking up something new. That's what set off the alarm."

"It looks like another portal," said Hudson, now able to study the scan data in more detail. His sense of panic had gone, but the excitement of the potential new discovery still set his pulse racing. He turned to Liberty. "Is this coming from your new invention down there?"

Liberty was still rapidly entering commands into her console and assimilating the data on her screen. "I think so," she said, between frenetic taps of the keyboard. "I think my little Frankenstein experiment might have actually worked."

Hudson sucked in a deep breath and let it out. He zoomed in on the location of the new contact and plotted its location in the system. "Whatever this new blip is, it's near the remains of what used to be the fourth planet in the system," said Hudson. "It's just an asteroid field now, though. If I remember rightly, the planet was presumed destroyed in a massive comet or asteroid collision sometime in the past."

When Liberty didn't respond, Hudson looked over to see her frowning down at her screen. It was more a look of apprehension than bewilderment, which was worrying enough that it prompted Hudson to check in with her.

"What's up, Liberty?" he asked, moving by her side. "You look pretty anxious for someone who may have just discovered the first new portal in decades."

Liberty glanced up at him and smiled, "I don't know what I'm feeling," she admitted, "and I also don't yet understand what I'm seeing." Liberty's screen was showing the same star chart from Hudson's navigation scanner. "This new blip, as you call it, is almost certainly a new portal," she went on, pointing to the new contact on her screen. "But its Shaak Radiation signature is uniquely different to all the other discovered portals, which is why we couldn't see it before."

"So, your little device down there has somehow tuned our scanners into this new frequency?" asked Hudson.

Liberty nodded, "The crystal seems able to detect a significantly wider spectrum of radiation frequencies. But it's more than just an ability to detect them, locally." She tapped in a sequence of commands and then waited as the display switched to a zoomed-out star chart. She pointed to a random selection of contacts that were overlaid on the chart as green chevrons. "These locations all correspond to the coordinates of known portals."

Hudson squinted down at the chart, and then frowned. He recognized many of the portal locations as destinations he'd visited before. "This is just existing map data, though, right?" asked Hudson. "Not a live feed?"

Liberty shook her head, "No, this is all live data."

"But how is that possible?" asked Hudson, as he counted the total number of green chevrons. It looked like every single known portal was being shown. "Some of these portals are thousands of light years from us, we couldn't possibly be picking them up."

Liberty shrugged, "I think our little crystalline discovery has redefined what's possible." Then she tapped away on the keypad again, adding, "But that isn't even the freakiest part." The star chart changed to show a number of new contacts, the markers distinguished from the original portal locations by a deep purple hue.

Hudson couldn't believe his eyes. "Wait a damn minute, are you telling me all of these purple blips are new portals?"

Liberty smiled and nodded. Hudson's knees almost buckled from underneath him, and he had to grab hold of the headrest of Liberty's chair to keep from toppling over. "This is incredible," he said, still struggling to process what he'd heard.

"This is the greatest discovery since Captain Shaak found the very first portal."

Liberty nodded again, "I know. I think, 'The Devan Portals' has a nice ring to it, don't you? Or, perhaps, 'The Liberty Worlds'?"

Hudson laughed, "You won't forget me when you're famous, will you?"

"I'm not making any promises" Liberty shrugged.

Hudson jostled Liberty on the shoulder, but then in his peripheral vision he was sure he caught something moving on the screen. "Did you see that?" he said to Liberty, as they both leaned in closer to the display.

Liberty nodded, "Yes, it looked like one of those blips moved."

"A moving portal would certainly be something new," replied Hudson. He was still staring intently at the screen, trying to spot the anomaly again. "We'd need to be careful to avoid those, or we could end up stranded in the ass end of the galaxy, permanently."

"There!" said Liberty, stabbing her finger on the screen. Hudson looked and saw another blip, but unlike the original portals, or the new purple-colored portals, this blip was red, and larger.

"Is that a portal, or something else?" wondered Hudson, feeling his mouth go dry.

Liberty zoomed in on the area where the red blip had appeared. However, along with some of the purple-colored portals, the red chevron was off the edge of the star chart. Hudson guessed that this meant the blip was a long way from any know region of space.

Hudson rubbed his eyes, and then deliberately forced himself to blink several times. "Is it just my eyes, or is that blip moving?"

Liberty leaned in even closer to the screen, and then quickly tapped another stream of commands into her console. "It's not your eyes; it's definitely moving. And it's also reading differently to the other portals, current and new."

Hudson sighed and felt the hairs on his neck tingle. His earlier feeling of being on a high was slowly seeping away, and being replaced by a shadowy sense of foreboding. "Do you think it's a third type of portal?" he asked.

Liberty shook her head, "I don't know. I don't think so. I'd need to study the data some more."

Then the red blip disappeared from the chart.

"Where the hell did it go?" said Hudson, starting again to feel a little panicky. There was a fine line between the excitement of a new discovery, and the fear of the unknown, he realized. It was like the fragile relationship between love and hate, except more sinister.

Liberty was busy tapping away at her console, her frown deepening by the second. "I don't know..." she finally answered, "maybe it really is just a blip. I mean, I did cobble together this thing out of scrap and junk from a curiosity shop."

Hudson was about to agree, when suddenly the red blip reappeared on the screen, but in a different location. "What the hell?" said Hudson, "It's back, but it's moved?"

Liberty zoomed the chart back out again and then checked the red blip's location, relative to its previous position. "It's definitely back, but from these new readings, it's perhaps five hundred light years away from where it was."

Hudson let out another sigh and rubbed his eyes. "Well, whatever the hell it is, it's still a long way from here. And, like you said, it's probably just a glitch."

Liberty sat back in her chair, still wearing an expression that was somewhere between anxious and excited. "I'll try to iron out the kinks later," she said, glancing over to Hudson. "The bigger question is, what do we do now?"

"Are you shitting me?" said Hudson, looking at her like she was crazy. "If your little blip detector is right, there's an undiscovered portal less than fifty million kilometers from where we are right now." Then he moved back over to the pilot's side of the cockpit and slid into his chair. "So, the next thing we do is find this portal and jump through it."

CHAPTER 23

Accelerating and decelerating at one-g for the duration of the journey, it had taken close to thirty-six hours to reach the coordinates indicated by Liberty's device. With Cutler still absent from their tail – though Hudson had a sneaking suspicion he hadn't gone far – there was no need to endure the discomfort of high-g travel.

This extra time had afforded them the chance to relax and recharge their batteries. And it had also allowed Liberty to work on her device, which she'd decided to call a 'scendar'. This stood for Shaak Crystal Energy Detection and Ranging, because of its similarities to Earth-based radar. However, unlike radar, Liberty's device didn't operate using radio waves, but something far more alien instead.

Despite Liberty's efforts to fine-tune the device, the scendar was still picking up the large, moving contact, indicated on the star chart by a red chevron. Worryingly, this contact, whether it was real or just a glitch, still appeared to be creeping ever closer to the network of known portal worlds.

However, Liberty had conceded that the blip had to remain a mystery for the time being. The Orion's deceleration burn had just completed, which meant they had finally arrived at the coordinates where an undiscovered portal potentially lay waiting. Both Liberty and Hudson were eager to discover whether their new portal was real or just another glitch in the scendar.

"Wow, this place is beautiful," said Liberty. She was staring out at the planetoid-sized fragments of what remained of Brahms Four. "If this was caused by an asteroid or comet collision, then it must have been one hell of a fireworks show."

"One best viewed from a safe distance," replied Hudson. "Say, two hundred thousand kilometers."

Liberty smiled and tapped a few commands into her keypad. "I've just sent you the most accurate coordinates for this mystery portal that I can glean from our navigation scanners," she said, staring back out at the fractured planet in front of them. "I guess we just fly at it and see what happens."

Hudson shrugged and nodded, "Not quite as dramatic as Captain Shaak's portal discovery, but I guess it will have to do," he said. Then he took hold of the ship's controls. "Moving us in now..."

Liberty watched the range decrease as Hudson teased the ship towards the location of the portal. As he got closer, he reduced their velocity and switched to thrusters only. There was arguably no need to approach so cautiously, but Hudson wasn't taking any chances.

"One thousand meters and closing," said Liberty, sounding breathless. "Adjust zero point five degrees to port... hold it there."

Hudson had never felt more nervous piloting a starship than he did at that moment. Even his final pilot's exam had felt less stressful. He found himself sucking in deep breaths and letting them out slowly, as if meditating.

"Two hundred meters..." said Liberty.

Hudson held his course. "Stand by for portal transition and main drive systems restart," he said, his voice quivering slightly. Then he looked over to Liberty, who was still strapped into her seat. "Don't you need to be in engineering to restart the drive systems?"

Liberty sat back and raised her eyebrows at him. "And miss the first discovery of a brand-new portal in generations? Not a chance in hell!"

Hudson understood her sentiment, but he still wished Liberty was in engineering. After all, they had no clue what would be on the other side of the portal. If they emerged into an asteroid field, or close to a black hole, or some other interstellar danger, they'd need their engines back up and running fast. However, if their roles were reversed, Hudson knew he wouldn't want to miss out either.

"Okay then, hold on to your seat," said Hudson. "Transition in five... four... three... two... one!"

Each of them held their breath. Hudson's hands had squeezed the control column and thruster control lever so tightly that his knuckles were white. Liberty's fingers were similarly taut, as she gripped the frame of her chair with more pressure than a crab's claw. Both waited. But then absolutely nothing happened.

"What the hell?" said Hudson, checking the coordinates. They were in the right place, but all they had travelled through was empty space. "Did we get the coordinates wrong?"

Liberty was busy tapping away at her keypad again, brow furrowed and eyes sharp. "These are the correct coordinates... I don't understand it." Then she glanced over at Hudson, "Bring us to a stop and swing us around; I'm going to try something."

Hudson did as Liberty requested, stopping their forward momentum and then pulsing the thrusters so that they were facing in the opposite direction. Then he watched as Liberty made some quick adjustments to the scendar device, before tapping at her keypad again.

"I had a thought on the way over here from Brahms Three," Liberty said. She had apparently predicted Hudson's imminent question concerning what she was doing. "I think these new portals are not just undiscovered – they're inactive."

"Inactive?" Hudson repeated. "You mean like a dormant volcano?"

"Not quite," replied Liberty. "The portal is still there, but the door hasn't been opened yet. Which means we need to ring the bell."

Hudson frowned. "As charming as your enigmatic descriptions are, this isn't a cryptic crossword club, Liberty. Can you tell me what you actually mean?"

"Fine, forget the analogies then," said Liberty, still working feverishly. "In simple terms, the crystal doesn't only receive, it can also transmit. Which means that if I can find the right resonant frequency to match this portal's Shaak Radiation signature..."

Hudson felt a reverberant thrum pulsing through the deck plating, and then the lights dimmed. In the gloom, he could see the alien crystal glowing brightly. He was about to alert Liberty, but then noticed on his status panel that the Orion was experiencing a massive power drain. He didn't know which incident to highlight first. However, he wasn't given the chance to warn Liberty about either, because there was a sudden, bright purple flash.

Hudson and Liberty both shielded their eyes as the intense, ethereal light flooded the cockpit. And then as quickly as it had appeared, it was gone.

Hudson checked the scendar device again, and the mysterious alien crystal had returned to its normal state. It was now merely passively reflecting the light in the cockpit. He checked his panel, and saw that the power drain had gone, but also that an additional five percent of their fuel reserves had too. He didn't have an explanation for any of it, but luckily, his plucky, genius engineer co-captain did.

"Ding-dong!" Liberty called out, beaming at him.

"Excuse me?" said Hudson.

"Ding-dong!" repeated Liberty, "As in ringing a doorbell. Come on, keep up, Hudson!"

Hudson rolled his eyes, "So is the damn door – I mean portal – open or not?"

"Only one way to find out..." replied Liberty, waving her hand towards the cockpit glass as if to beckon Hudson forward.

Hudson blew out a sigh and shook his head. "This had better work, otherwise I have another thirty-six hours in deep space back to Brahms Three, with only your crappy jokes to amuse me..." He then pushed the thruster control forward and started to creep the Orion back towards where the portal was supposed to be. The tension and excitement had somehow now dissipated, making the event bizarrely anti-climactic.

"Three hundred meters..." said Liberty, again anxiously watching her instruments. For her, at least, it appeared no less exciting. "Two hundred... one hundred..."

Then there was another bright purple flash, followed by a swirling pattern of dancing light and energy. It was a display that Hudson was intimately familiar with, having seen it dozens of times before; they were transiting though a portal. Then, mere seconds later, they were back in deep space again. However, this time there wasn't the broken remains of a planet in front of them, but a vivid, light blue orb that shone with the reflected light of a new yellow star. Hudson and Liberty both just sat there, mouths gaping open, staring at the new world. It could have been seconds or minutes before one of them spoke. Finally, Liberty eventually snapped out of her trance and checked her instruments.

"It's a rocky, terrestrial-like planet," said Liberty, her voice uncharacteristically shaky. "Vegetative life for sure, looking at the spectra, but other than that, I can't be sure from here."

Hudson tested the controls; thrusters were responding, but the main drive system was down. It was the same as any other portal transition. Then he glanced down at the navigation scanner and could hardly believe what he saw.

"Liberty, take a look at where we are," he said, double checking the readings.

Liberty frowned down at the readout and then ran some distance calculations, based on their location relative to all of the other known portal positions. "Wow, no-one has ever been out this far, or to this part of the galaxy." Then she beamed at Hudson, "Captain Shaak, eat your heart out!"

Hudson laughed, but then the strange red chevron appeared again on the scanner. The hairs on the back of his neck tingled, sucking the joy out of him like a black hole eating light. He knew he'd need to tackle the subject of what this was sooner or later, or it would drive him insane. However, for now, they had more important matters to attend to. Namely, exploring the brand-new star system and planet in front of them.

"You'll never guess what else I'm detecting," teased Liberty.

"A sense of humility?" joked Hudson, but Liberty merely stared back at him, unimpressed.

"No... I'm detecting a Shaak Radiation signature from the planet."

Hudson sat up in his seat, "You mean there's an alien wreck on the planet's surface?"

Liberty nodded, "I think so, but we'll need to go down there to investigate. It's an oxygen-nitrogen atmosphere, a little nitrogen rich, but breathable. And gravity of zero-point-nine-four-g."

Hudson huffed a laugh. It still blew his mind that all of the planets at the other end of the portals were essentially Earth-like worlds. There had to be a reason, he assumed, but like so many other unexplained phenomena connected to the alien wrecks, it remained a mystery.

"What are you waiting for?" asked Liberty, snapping Hudson out of his daydream. "Let's get down there!"

"Oh, I'd love to," replied Hudson, folding his arms and looking smug. "But, aren't you forgetting something?"

Liberty thought for a moment, but then frowned and shrugged. "Please?"

Hudson laughed and slapped his thighs. "The politeness is appreciated, Liberty, but what I mean is, you need to re-start our drive systems first..."

CHAPTER 24

Both of them gazed over the horizon of the new world from their vantage point on the outer hull of the alien wreck. The Orion gleamed in the near distance, under the warm light of the yellow sun. Hudson had set the ship down about a hundred meters from the hulking vessel, which protruded from the rocky landscape like a thorn. It was the only blot on what otherwise ranked amongst the most spectacular terrain Hudson had ever laid eyes on. Jagged mountains rose out of the plains like giant, broken teeth, with rivers that put the Amazon to shame snaking between them. Three small moons hung above them in the hazy orange sky, each as stunning to behold as the landscape that surrounded them. But despite the planet's jaw-dropping beauty, the most striking aspect about it was the lack of civilization.

"I'm so used to seeing busy spaceports and bustling scavenger towns built up around wrecks like this one," said Hudson. He was spinning around and around, soaking in the atmosphere. "It looks almost unreal without it, and somehow much more alien."

"And so much more beautiful," Liberty added, smiling at him.

Hudson nodded and returned the smile. He realized then that Liberty was seeing the world through the exact same lens as he was. They were both experiencing something that no other human being had done in many decades. The last person to set foot on a new, alien world had died long before either of them had even been born. And now, here they both were – discoverers of the first new alien wreck in generations.

"We should get inside the wreck, and see what we can score," said Liberty, scanning the outer hull for openings.

Hudson sucked in a deep breath of the fresh, cool alien air. "Don't be in such a hurry, Liberty," he said, enjoying the comforting heat of the sun on his face. "Take a minute to soak all of this in. Every last drop." Then he looked over at her. "And never forget it. Because these are the moments we live for, Liberty. And they may never come again."

Liberty nodded and moved back beside Hudson, hooking her arm through his. For several minutes they just stood together on the alien wreck, as the cool breeze washed over them.

"How long before they build one of those awful scavenger towns out here?" said Liberty.

Hudson laughed. "Probably not long."

"I hope it won't be as big a shit-hole as the one on Brahms Three," added Liberty. "I don't want them messing up my planet with sleazy clubs and container-lined streets."

"I know how you feel," replied Hudson. "But at least we got to see it like this first." Then his smile turned more mischievous and his eyes grew wider. "And do you know what else we get first?"

Liberty grinned; she already knew what Hudson was hinting at, and what the answer to his question was too. "We get to pick all the low-hanging fruit!"

"And, even better, there's no RGF to steal it from us," added Hudson.

"Not yet, anyway," Liberty was quick to caveat. "The flash from the portal opening sent out a pretty powerful Shaak Radiation burst. That will probably already have been detected at Brahms Three."

"Shit, I hadn't considered that," admitted Hudson. "At two or three gs, it might only be maybe ten or twelve hours before someone else pops up here. And it wouldn't surprise me if that someone wore the black and blue uniform of the RGF."

"In that case, we'd better get to work..." agreed Liberty. "The problem is, how do we get inside this thing? On the other wrecks, there are already bridges and platforms to help hunters reach a suitable entry point."

"All part of hunting out on the frontier, Liberty!" replied Hudson, enthusiastically. "I suggest we check the hull at ground level first. Hopefully we can find a convenient entry location."

Liberty nodded, and started to lead the way down from their vantage point on the hull. "All of the most valuable relics tend to be found deeper inside the wrecks," she said, hopping over the crumbled deck plates, like scrambling over rocks.

"It's probably best if we don't venture too far inside this time," said Hudson, adding a note of caution. "We don't want to end up like our bony friend, Percy Harrison."

Liberty appeared to physically shudder at the memory of the relic hunter that had perished in the wreck on Bach Two. "Good point..."

The wreck on the new, unnamed world was much the same as the others Hudson had seen. It was part-buried in the ground, at the end of an enormous trench that had been carved into the landscape after the ship had crashed to the surface. As such, there were natural openings in the hull, where the force of the impact, and collisions with mountains and rocky features had ripped through the thick armor. However, it still took them almost two hours to find an opening that was deep enough to lead into the ship's internal structure. And also one that was safe enough to traverse without risking a grisly death.

Hudson finished fixing one of the self-attaching pitons into the alien metal above his head, and then tossed the rope back to Liberty. "Last one, and then we're inside," he said, pressing his hands to his hips and blowing out heavily.

Liberty caught the rope and then swung over beside Hudson, noting that his breathing was labored. "You've spent too much time sitting on your backside, flying starships..." she commented, grinning.

Hudson smiled, "Relic hunting is certainly a lot easier when the ropes and ladders are already in place," he said. Then he pointed along the freshly exposed internal corridor. "Now, if you're quite finished insulting my fitness, do something useful and scout ahead down that corridor."

Liberty switched on her headtorch and also turned on a string of LED strips attached to the straps of her rucksack. "Whatever you say, skipper," she replied, jogging ahead.

Hudson sucked in another few breaths and then followed, but at a much steadier pace. "Now you're just showing off..." he called after her. However Hudson didn't have to go far before he caught up with Liberty. "Catching your breath too?" he said, reaching her side, before it then became obvious why she had stopped. Blocking the corridor was an enormous sphere, with hexagonal dimples in the surface that made it resemble a giant metal golf-ball.

"What the hell is this thing?" said Hudson, moving closer to the object and running his hand along the dimpled surface. "I've never seen or heard of anything like this before."

Liberty had placed her rucksack on the ground and was pulling out an assortment of tools. "That's probably because you're not an engineering nerd, like me," she said, smoothing back a loose tuft of her blue-streaked hair. Then she selected one of the tools and began working on the metal sphere. "I read about them in some of the alien tech research journals," she continued, as a panel on the surface of the sphere started to come loose. "There was never any consensus on what they are," she continued. "But the idea I liked the most was that they were sort of worker drones."

Hudson moved behind Liberty to provide some additional light from his headtorch, and also to get a better view of what she was doing. "You mean like for repair and maintenance?"

Liberty nodded, "The idea was that these things rolled around inside the corridors, moving to whichever part of the ship needed fixing up." Then she pulled the panel away and tossed it to the ground. Inside, the sphere was largely hollow, with the exterior panels connected to a central core.

She pointed inside, "It looks like it can sort of reconfigure itself, like a hyper-sophisticated swiss army knife." She then swapped the tool in her hand for two others that she'd already laid out next to her rucksack, and leant inside the object.

"Hey, be careful," said Hudson, worried that the object might swallow her whole.

"Don't worry," replied Liberty, head and upper body inside the device, as if she was working on a truck engine. "Academics might disagree on what this thing is, but we do know what they contain." Then she reappeared, holding a metal sphere about the size of a pumpkin. She prized it open, using one of the tools. "The reason you never see these is that they're the first things to get stripped down in a wreck."

Hudson peered inside and blew out a long, low whistle. "That's some sort of processor core, right?" Liberty nodded, and then started to lever out several components from inside. "There should be at least one high-grade CPU shard in here, and some lower-grade secondary cores, plus some other good kit too. This thing alone makes it worth the trip."

Suddenly, Hudson felt like he'd gotten a second wind. "Is there anything I can do?"

"Yeah, if you're feeling energetic," replied Liberty, without looking up from the spherical device. "The metal panels that cover this thing are made of an alien super-metal that beats anything human scientists have come up with by several orders of magnitude. It's melted down and used to make alloys for starship hull plating – the Orion has some of it on its hull."

"Doesn't seem like the amount here will go very far," said Hudson. He then dusted his hands and set to work stripping the panels from the sphere. "This lot wouldn't even cover the dorsal section of the Orion."

Liberty popped out one of the secondary CPU shards from the device she was working on, and slipped it into her rucksack. "You only need a small amount, mixed into an alloy with existing metals. It's really funky stuff, and self-healing too. It's why I didn't need to patch-up the ding in the hull after Cutler winged us. It repaired itself."

Hudson laughed, and then yanked another panel loose, before dropping it onto the growing pile. "In that case, maybe we keep a panel or two at Ma's safehouse. Because I doubt it's the last time we'll get shot at by that shit-for-brains."

"What a happy thought," said Liberty, dropping another CPU shard into the bag.

They both continued to work for another two hours, until they had stripped all that they could realistically carry in their two rucksacks. Then they had cautiously made their way back outside the ship and stashed the relics in the Orion's hold.

By that point, the sun had started to set over the jagged, rocky horizon. They reluctantly agreed to call it a day for their relic-hunting activities. Hudson knew there was more low-hanging fruit to grab, but it was treacherous work, and he didn't want to risk either of them getting injured. And there was still also the chance that the RGF or the CET could descend on them the next morning, or even a rival hunter crew. He didn't want to get caught on the hop. It was bad enough facing off against other hunters in the existing wrecks, which were patrolled by the RGF. Out in the lawless, virgin territory of this newly-discovered planet, there would be nothing to stop an unscrupulous crew from stealing their score. From what he'd seen, he wouldn't even put it past a crew to steal their ship and leave them stranded. However, quite apart from all of those good reasons, Hudson was worn-out, and ravenously hungry. Liberty looked similarly frazzled.

Instead of eating inside the ship, Liberty had suggested sitting outside and watching the sun go down. And though Hudson had initially poo-pooed the idea as poetic nonsense, he'd eventually agreed. He was glad he had done. It wasn't that Hudson had never seen a sunset before – he'd seen hundreds, across dozens of worlds – but this had put them all to shame. Whether it was tiredness, the four shots of Ma's special whiskey, or just the sheer beauty of it, he didn't know, but he'd found himself wiping a tear from his eye.

Liberty appeared to have noticed this, and was observing him out of the corner of her eye, lips curled into an amused smirk. Hudson knew she was getting ready to gloat about how right she had been to suggest they sit outside. To save himself from her, 'I told you so' self-righteousness, he quickly pushed himself up and started walking towards a rocky outcrop behind the ship.

"Where are you off to?" Liberty called out after him "You do realize that there are no bars in this scavenger town?"

"I'm going to take a leak, if you must know," Hudson called back, inventing a reason on the spot. Though now that he'd said it, he did find himself needing to go.

"No peeing on the landing struts," he heard her reply, but he was already past the ship and climbing up onto the rocks. He was about to reach for his flies, when he saw something glinting under the light of the planet's multiple moons. He frowned and scrambled down the other side of the rocks to get a closer look. The object was covered in a blanket of dusty soil that had the effect of camouflaging it, like a stingray hiding under the sand. Hudson brushed some of the soil away and discovered that the object was made from the same sort of metal as the alien hulk. Except it was on a far smaller scale. Part of it appeared to be buried in the ground, but Hudson estimated that it was still no larger than the Orion, and probably even smaller.

"Hey, Liberty, you might want to take a look at this!" Hudson yelled back.

There was a brief pause, before Liberty shouted, "Don't be so bloody disgusting!"

Hudson rolled his eyes, "No, I don't mean my..." then he stopped, realizing he was only making things worse, and instead yelled out. "Just get your ass over here, will you?"

Hudson heard the disgruntled trudge of Liberty's boots on the ground, as if even the way she walked communicated her annoyance. Then she finally appeared on the rocks above him.

"What do you want?" she said, folding her arms. "I was comfy back there."

Hudson just gestured to the object in front of him, and then started to dust off more of its surface. Liberty practically fell off the rock she was standing on, and scrambled down to Hudson's side. She dusted off more of the surface, inspecting it as if she'd just uncovered an extremely rare and valuable classic car in a scrapyard.

"Do you think it's a chunk of the main hulk that fell off as it crashed?" Hudson asked.

Liberty shook her head, "No, it's the same material, but the design is different and those are clearly engines at the rear. Plus, if you look closely, these panels are smaller, more intricate. Whatever this is, it was built this size."

"Then it has to be another ship, right?" said Hudson. "An alien shuttle perhaps?"

Liberty was bustling around the object with such vitality that she was almost glowing. "I don't know, but that's as good a guess as any. If it is, it's the first of its kind ever discovered." She ran up to Hudson, "Do you know what this means?"

Hudson nodded, "Yes, it means tonight's relic hunting expedition isn't over yet." Then he turned away from Liberty and walked over to the rocks.

Liberty pressed her hands to her hips. "Where the hell are you going? The ship is over here." Then she heard the sound of a zipper being undone.

"Unless you want me to wet myself inside that new alien ship, can you let me have a damn pee first?"

CHAPTER 25

While Hudson relieved himself against the rocks, Liberty had hurried back to the Orion to get her tools. She had then occupied herself with the task of finding an entrance into the mysterious alien ship. There had not been an obvious hatch or door, at least not one that matched what she'd expect to see on a human-designed ship. However, towards the rear third of what she assumed was the top of the vessel, there was a single hexagonal panel about a meter wide. It was unique in that it was the only panel of that shape that she had found on the exposed sections of the hull. She had also commented that It reminded her of the hexagonal corridors in the larger hulk nearby.

"If you've finished watering the plants, I could really use a hand about now," Liberty called out to Hudson.

"I finished ages ago, I'm not a damn elephant," Hudson called back. He had actually been scouting around the edge of the ship for the last couple of minutes, clearing off the debris and moving some of the smaller rocks. He climbed up onto the hull and approached Liberty. "Remarkably, the ship actually looks intact," he said, crouching down by her side and looking at the panel. "Whatever this thing is made of must be pretty tough."

"It's the same metal that the spherical drone was covered with, except much thicker, by the looks of it," said Liberty. "If the Orion was plated in this stuff, we'd be able to stand toe-to-toe with a CET Destroyer or an MP Gunboat."

"Neither prospect really appeals," said Hudson, "but I get your point." Then he tapped on the hexagonal panel. "Is this our way in?"

Liberty handed Hudson a small hatchet. He took it but then raised an eyebrow at her. "What am I supposed to do with this? Hack my way through?"

"Good luck with that," replied Liberty. "No, I just need you to prize up a corner when you see it pop open."

Then Liberty removed an alien power cell from her rucksack, plus a few additional leads and components that Hudson didn't recognize. "I'm going to try to hotwire it." She pointed to a small hexagonal indentation just below the panel. "I've seen these before, or read about them anyway. If you pump enough alien juice into them, it triggers the hatch. It's how the early relic hunters managed to open some sealed corridors on the wrecks."

"Well, I for one am grateful for all the reading you do," said Hudson as Liberty worked to attach the devices. "I never get much past the cartoons in the daily epaper."

"You do surprise me..." said Liberty, without attempting to hide the sarcasm. "Okay, get ready, I'm going to activate the power cell in three... two... one... now!"

Liberty activated the cell and suddenly the edges of the hexagonal panel began to glow. Hudson pressed the blade of the hatchet into the seam, ready to lever it open. But instead of the hatch popping outward, it dropped down and then rapidly retracted inside the ship. The blade of the hatchet slid into the opening, and with it went Hudson, face first into the ship. He fell for less than a second, but the impact still felt like he'd been hit by a truck.

"Hudson!" Liberty shouted into the opening. "Hudson, are you okay?"

Hudson groaned and rubbed the back of his head. Luckily, he hadn't impaled himself on the blade of the hatchet, which now glinted under the moonlight streaming in from outside.

"Yeah, I'm okay," said Hudson, wearily. "I take it back; this was a stupid idea."

"Well, it *was* your idea," said Liberty, smirking, before tossing a rope through the hole. It hit

Hudson on the head, and he glowered back up at her. He would have protested more verbally, but he was aware that he needed Liberty to get him out again. "I'm going to secure the other end of the rope around a rock. Don't go anywhere..." Her head disappeared from outside the hatch.

Hudson laughed. *Don't go anywhere. What a wise ass...* Then he grabbed a flashlight from his belt and started to search around the inside of the ship. If it *was* a ship, it didn't resemble any kind of vessel that Hudson had seen before. The interior walls were hexagonal, like in the main hulk, but there was no discernable cockpit and it all appeared to be on one level. The section behind him, towards where the engines protruded above ground, was blocked. He tapped on the wall with his flashlight, but there was no obvious way through. Instead, he edged forward, sliding down towards the front of the ship that was buried beneath the rocky soil. He could see some evidence of damage now, including blown-out conduits and twisted panels, but the hull still appeared intact.

Sweeping his flashlight from side-to-side as he moved cautiously forward, Hudson caught a glimpse of an object directly in his path. Edging more slowly towards it, he discovered a sphere, nestled in a small indentation, like an egg. Protruding from it, into the hull above and around it, were metal pillars. It reminded him of the room in the hulk on Bach Two, where Cutler had tried to kill him for the second time. In that room there had also been a central sphere with a similar arrangement of metal pillars. The only significant difference was that the one he was looking at now was many times smaller, and more ornate. It could have sat in a museum and drawn interested crowds, Hudson mused.

Hudson checked behind to see if there was any sign of Liberty, but she hadn't returned. He considered waiting for her, since she was the engineering expert, but curiosity got the better of him. Sliding down to the sphere, he began to inspect it more closely. It resembled the processor core from the center of the drone that they'd stripped earlier, but at least three times the size. Then he noticed that a panel on the top appeared to be loose. He shone the flashlight onto it and lifted it with his hand, but the panel flexed like a sheet of cooked lasagna. "What the hell is this?" Hudson wondered out loud, peering inside the device, but it was again like nothing he'd seen before. Checking back a second time, he saw Liberty slowly sliding down the rope. *I'd better leave this to her to suss out...* he reasoned, reminding himself of the several times he'd sassily warned Liberty not to blow them up. However, the urge to poke around inside it was still too strong.

He held back the flexible panel with the end of his torch and then slid his hand inside the sphere.

It felt almost liquid, like the toy goop that kids can buy from novelty stores. Then his finger touched something solid, and he felt and heard a click. A second later, the sphere illuminated like a light bulb, and a cavernous thrum started to build up inside the ship. He yanked his hand out of the goop and the flexible panel slid off the torch and sealed the gap, as if drawn by a powerful magnetic force. Hudson scrambled back as the thin metal arms protruding out of the sphere started to shift, detaching from their positions in the wall and making new connections. Hudson had seen enough. He turned and ran.

"Liberty, we have to get out!" he called to her, struggling to make the climb back to the rope.

"What? I just got here!" protested Liberty. Then the whole ship started to quake, violently. Ahead, the gloom began to dissolve as the sphere grew ever brighter. "What did you do?" shrieked Liberty, eyes wide with fear.

"I'll tell you later," replied Hudson, "But we have to get out, right now!"

Hudson climbed the rope first, adrenalin fueling his aching muscles. When he reached the top, he started to pull the line out, hauling Liberty with it, though she too was climbing at a furious speed. *Come on, come on!* Hudson cried out in his mind. If the hatch closed with Liberty still inside, there was no telling what would happen to her. Liberty held out a hand as her head poked out of the opening, and Hudson reached down and grabbed it. With all of his strength, he hauled her out of the alien ship, and the blink of an eye later the hatch slammed shut like the blade of a guillotine.

Both of them scrambled off the hull, practically falling the last couple of meters to the dusty soil below. Then they ran, putting as much distance between themselves and the alien ship as they could, until they collapsed from exhaustion. The effort of the climb and the sprint, on top of a day's hard relic-hunting, was just too much. They turned over and lay on their backs, watching as the engines of the alien ship roared into life. Then, slowly at first, the vessel lifted itself out of its grave, shaking off dirt and rock like a songbird shaking off water.

Hudson and Liberty were frozen in fear and awe, as the ship lifted higher and higher, the noise from its power core rising in time with its altitude. And then its engines glowed brighter, and it sped away over the horizon, disappearing into the night.

CHAPTER 26

Neither Hudson nor Liberty said a word for several minutes. At first, they just rested on the dirt, gasping for breath, trying to feed their brains with enough oxygen to process what had happened. However, there were no words that could aptly describe what they'd just witnessed. To talk about it would almost seem to diminish the magnitude of the event. Yet Hudson knew that he and Liberty had to face up to it soon, and more importantly, decide what to do next. Humanity may have come to terms with the notion of other worlds and broken alien starships, but this was another matter entirely. There was a universe of difference between crashed hulks on distant, empty worlds, and a living alien threat.

Hudson knew it was an assumption to believe the alien ship posed a danger. Nevertheless, of all the sensations that had flooded through his body upon seeing the vessel take off, terror was by far the most deep rooted of them.

"What should we do now?" asked Liberty.

She hadn't sounded panicked or even afraid, but her voice still came across as unusually cheerless. It was also an interesting first question, Hudson thought, and not the one he had expected from her. He'd anticipated questions centered on what the ship was, where it might be going, how it operated... But her actual question had been the right one to ask. It was just unfortunate that Hudson had no clue how to answer.

"I think we'd better get off this rock, as quickly as we can," he replied, thinking discretion was the better part of valor. He looked over at her, seeing the same apprehension behind her eyes that he was sure shone in his own. "I don't really want to still be around if it decides to come back and find out who woke it up."

Liberty nodded, and neither of them spoke again for a few seconds. Both were keenly watching the horizon but, bar the gradual flow of wispy clouds, it was still. If it hadn't been for the crater left behind, Hudson could have almost believed that the alien ship had never existed.

"What happened in there?" asked Liberty. Unlike her outburst inside the alien ship, this time the question hadn't sounded like an accusation.

Hudson sighed and shook his head. He could describe the events as they unfolded, but he didn't have an explanation for any of it.

"I found a sphere; like the one you dug out of that drone, except bigger," Hudson began. "It was hooked into the ship like the thing we saw on Bach Two, where Cutler jumped us. But it was also different. The metal on the outside was flexible, like fabric." He was struggling to articulate it in a way that didn't sound dumb, but Liberty didn't question him, and continued to listen with intense interest. "And then inside, it was almost fluid. Amorphous. I touched something, and it came... alive."

"Alive?" repeated Liberty.

"That's the only way I can describe it," replied Hudson. "But there was no cockpit inside the ship, and no instruments or console screens. Hell, there weren't even any damn chairs. I can't explain it."

Liberty exhaled and then frowned, but it was a look of deep concentration, rather than confusion or skepticism. Hudson had learned to recognize her different looks by now. "A living ship. But inorganic," she offered. Then she looked up at Hudson, and added. "An artificial intelligence?"

Hudson sucked in his lips and shrugged, "It's as good a guess as any."

Hudson's answer, though non-committal, since he couldn't confirm Liberty's suspicion one way or another, seemed to rally her spirits. However, almost as quickly as her vitality had returned, it ebbed again.

"Do you think..." she began, but then hesitated, swallowing hard, before continuing. "Do you think it might be hostile?"

This had been the question that burned inside Hudson's mind since the moment the spherical object had burst into life. Assuming it was alive.

"We have to consider that possibility," Hudson answered. He decided that honesty was preferable to making Liberty feel better with a comforting piece of conjecture. "But I've never believed that these alien wrecks just crashed by accident. Something must have taken them all down, and that something wasn't friendly." Then he turned around, slowly taking in the landscape of the breathtaking new world again. "Humanity has hopped from portal to portal, world to world, for so long that it was only a matter of time before our luck ran out. Maybe we've finally caught up with whatever caused all this destruction in the first place."

"I was kind of just looking for a reassuring lie, if I'm honest," said Liberty, with a weak smile. "But I guess burying our heads in the sand isn't going to help either of us."

"Well, whatever it was, I know that I don't want to be here if it comes back," said Hudson, turning back to the Orion. Liberty followed a couple of paces behind, but then the sky cracked like thunder. They both peered up, urgently trying to locate what had caused the noise.

"Is it the alien ship?" asked Liberty, spinning on her heels.

Hudson too was wheeling around, but then he spotted the source of the sonic boom. It was a ship, but it wasn't the alien shuttle. He recognized the shape immediately as an RGF Patrol Craft. And it wasn't alone; pursuing it was a much larger CET Gunboat.

"We've got company, but it's not aliens," said Hudson, pointing up into the sky. "I almost wish it was, but it's worse."

Liberty glanced up to the area of sky where Hudson was pointing and spotted the two ships. She pressed her hands to her hips and shook her head. "You have got to be kidding me..."

CHAPTER 27

The RGF Patrol Craft circled around Hudson and Liberty, as they waited beside the Orion. Then a voice blared out over the public address system from the ship. "Relic hunter crew, hold your position. Do not attempt to depart or you will be fired upon."

"I guess that answers our question about whether or not to get out of here," said Liberty, still with her hands on her hips.

Hudson didn't answer; there was something about the voice he found familiar, and it gave him a sinking feeling.

The patrol craft landed first, setting down about twenty meters from the Orion, while the much larger CET Gunboat descended further away. Even so, the downdraught from its landing thrusters still almost knocked them from their feet.

"Do we tell them about the alien ship?" asked Liberty, as the rear ramp of the RGF Patrol Craft lowered.

"I wouldn't tell those RGF bastards anything," replied Hudson, "especially not about our score."

"But they can't tax us, can they?" asked Liberty. From the incredulous tone of her voice, Hudson knew she had only just considered that possibility. In contrast, it was the first thought Hudson had after seeing the Patrol Craft in the sky.

"I have no doubt they will try, but we stick to our guns, okay?" said Hudson, and Liberty nodded. "As for the alien ship, let's see if we can get a chance to speak to the CET captain alone. Assuming he's not a massively stuck-up asshole, that is."

"How likely is that?" asked Liberty.

Hudson laughed, "I guess you've not met many CET captains?"

The condescending tone didn't sit well with Liberty. "You know, they don't tend to frequent boneyards, unlike washed-out, ex-RGF cops, anyway..."

Hudson smiled and nudged her with his elbow, "Ouch, that one hurt." However, his jocular mood soon soured when he saw who was approaching out of the back of the patrol craft.

"I don't believe it," groaned Liberty, who had evidently also seen the RGF officer approaching. "What is it with this guy?"

"Well, well, well, if it isn't Hudson Powell," said Logan Griff, stopping a few meters in front of them. Then his eyes flicked over to Liberty. He looked her up and down, stroking his wiry moustache with his forefinger and thumb as he did so. "And the delectable Liberty Devan. It's nice to see *you* again..." he added, as his eyes washed over her for a second time.

"The feeling isn't mutual," replied Liberty, "and if you don't take your filthy eyes off me, I'm going to gouge them out of your thick skull."

Griff's expression hardened, "One day, you'll regret talking to me like that, girl," he growled, before turning back to Hudson. "I've been following your progress with interest, rook. I've never seen anyone evade Cutler's grasp for so long. I'm almost impressed."

"I don't care what you think, shit head," replied Hudson, sharply. "Now what do you want? Because we were about to leave."

Griff tutted and wagged a finger at Hudson. "Oh no, I'm afraid not. I first need to take a look in your hold, and see what untaxed relics you've taken from the lovely new wreck you discovered." Then he slow-clapped, sarcastically. "Well done, by the way. You're going to be the most famous dead relic hunter in the galaxy, once Cutler catches up with you again."

Hudson stepped up to Griff, and jabbed a finger into his sternum, making him stagger back. "You need to hire a better hitman. Or have the guts to face me yourself." Griff's hand went to his sidearm, but Hudson quickly pulled back the lapel of his leather jacket to reveal the pistol. "I wouldn't try that, if I were you."

"You can't stop me from taking your score, rook," said Griff, growing angrier by the second. You're a licensed hunter. You owe a percentage to the RGF, whether you like it or not. And you can't stop me taking my slice too."

Hudson gestured to the landscape surrounding them. "I don't see any checkpoint scanners, asshole," he said. Then he peered into Griff's eyes again, "And I don't give a shit if you're RGF, CET or Santa Claus himself. You set one foot in my ship, and you'll walk out again on crutches."

The scrunch of bootsteps on the gravelly soil interrupted their bitter exchange. Hudson glanced past Griff to see two CET military officers approaching.

Griff quickly looked behind and spotted them too, before glowering back at Hudson. "We'll see about that, rook," he snarled, as he backed away, and waited for the CET officers to come alongside.

Liberty moved up next to Hudson, watching the two CET officers closely. "What do you reckon? Is he a massively stuck-up asshole captain or not?"

"Oh, shit..." Hudson answered, drawing an inquisitive frown from Liberty. "We are honored," he added, glancing back at her. "There's not just a captain, but a full-blown commodore too."

The CET officers strode past Griff without even acknowledging him. And from the look on Griff's gaunt, lined face, it was clear he'd taken offence. The older of the two officers then approached Hudson and stretched out his hand. He was a late middle-aged man, with short, brown hair that was tinged silver at the tips around his ears. Hudson could judge something about a person by how they moved. And unlike Logan Griff, whose lanky gait and slippery persona showed in the way he seemed to ooze from place to place, the commodore's movement flowed openly and organically. He lacked the regimental stiffness that most of the CET officers Hudson had met seemed to possess.

"I'm Commodore Elias Trent, from the Coalition of Earth Territories central command," the man announced as Hudson took his hand and shook it. Then he indicated to the VCX-110 behind them. "I assume you are Captain Hudson of the Orion?"

"Co-captain, actually," said Hudson, looking at Liberty. "I'm Hudson Powell, and this is Liberty Devan."

Commodore Trent appeared embarrassed and immediately offered a hand to Liberty. "Apologies, I should not have presumed," he said, sounding genuinely repentant.

Liberty took the hand that was offered. "No, you shouldn't have, but apology accepted, thank you."

Trent smiled and then addressed them both. "Well, congratulations are in order," he said, taking a long look at the planet's striking scenery. "The first new portal and portal world discovered in over sixty years. Quite remarkable; I never thought I would stand on a brand-new world in my lifetime."

Hudson smiled, finding himself actually liking the commodore, which was unexpected. "I don't think anyone did, least of all us. I also didn't expect a commodore to be greeting us."

Trent laughed, "I wouldn't have missed it for the world, or any worlds," he said. Then he pointed to the gunboat in the distance. "So, I commandeered the fastest ship I could get hold of and came out as quickly as I could." Then he rubbed his neck and added, "Though I'm getting a little old for sustained high-g travel, these days."

Griff now stepped forward again, "I hate to break up this lovely moment, but can we return to the matter at hand? Namely, how did these two degenerates find the portal that led here."

Trent looked at Griff as if he was a raw recruit that had just forgotten to salute. "A question that is of no concern to the Relic Guardian Force, corporal," he said, sternly. "Your role here is simply to survey the site, map the perimeter for the checkpoint district, and secure the wreck." Griff stared back at Trent with similar contempt, but he was smart enough to keep his mouth shut. A commodore enjoyed broad authority, and since this new world fell under the jurisdiction of the CET, the planet was effectively under the governorship of Trent. "It will be another four days before the engineering crews arrive to begin construction of the settlement. In that time, the RGF's role is simply to prevent the wreck from being looted."

Griff's face reddened, but he bit his tongue, before turning from Trent to Hudson. "Speaking of looting, we need to inspect and recover the relics that these two have already stolen."

Griff took a step towards the Orion, but Trent raised his arm to bar his progress. "You will do no such thing," said Trent. Hudson was grateful for his intervention, because a second later and he would have blocked Griff's path himself, but with far less restraint than Trent had shown. "The tradition is to allow those who discover a new wreck first-finder rights. Whatever they have already found will not be taxed by the CET," then he paused and added with more gravitas, "or the Relic Guardian Force."

"You don't have the authority..." Griff began, but then he stopped, realizing his mistake.

Trent turned and squared off against the lanky RGF officer. Hudson realized then that Trent was almost as tall as Griff, but at least two weight

225

classes above him, making Griff look weedy in comparison. "Yes, I do," he said smoothly. Then he read the name badge on Griff's jacket. "Now, Corporal Logan Griff, you will attend to your duties, and bother this hunter crew no more, or I will be speaking to your superiors. Is that understood?"

Griff gritted his teeth, biting down hard to stop himself from saying something he'd surely regret. Then he backed away, jabbing a nicotine-stained finger at Hudson. "I'll see you soon," he snarled, before glancing at Liberty and blowing her a kiss. If it hadn't been for the fact that Griff's back had already been turned, Hudson was sure Liberty would have somersaulted over the top of Trent's head and stomped Griff's smug face into the dirt.

"My apologies for the rudeness of the RGF officer," said Trent. "I'm afraid I've yet to meet one of their kind who doesn't merit being airlocked into space."

Hudson and Liberty both laughed. The joke had expertly relieved the tension. "Don't worry, we're used to it," replied Hudson. "But thanks."

"I'm afraid this wreck is now off-limits until the checkpoint district has been established," Trent continued. "But something tells me that this won't be the only new portal you two discover."

Hudson shrugged and acted coy. "Who knows?"

"Don't worry, I won't press you for your secrets," said Trent, holding up his hands. "But news of this discovery has travelled fast, as have your names. I expect that wherever you go from here, you may have a convoy in tow. As wonderful as this new discovery is, I'm afraid it has also painted a target on your backs. So please be careful."

Hudson hadn't considered this, but now that Trent had mentioned it, he realized he was right. The next portal they uncovered would result in a much more hotly contested gold rush. Worse still, the more mercenary hunters might even make a play for the Orion, or Liberty's scendar device. "Thanks for the heads-up, and the advice," he said, before glancing over at Liberty. "We'll make sure we and the ship are well prepared for such eventualities."

"Good, then for now I shall leave you," said Trent. "Though I suspect it will not be the last time I hear your names."

Trent turned to leave, but then Hudson remembered about the alien shuttle. With Griff's appearance, he'd forgotten about it, but now the frightening memory crept back into his mind. Trent had seemed trustworthy, and Hudson felt that he could confide in him, without fear of blame or repercussions.

"Commodore, wait," said Hudson, causing the senior officer to halt and twist his head back. "There's something else we need to mention." Then Hudson glanced at the CET captain, who had not been introduced. The younger man presented the appearance of stuck-up snootiness that Hudson was used to seeing from the CET. "Alone, if possible," Hudson added.

Trent's thick eyebrows lifted up, but then he turned to the unnamed captain and dismissed him. The officer shot a snooty, affronted look at Hudson and then marched away.

Hudson waited until the captain was well out of earshot and then closed the distance between him and Trent, with Liberty alongside.

"I'm all ears, Captains Powell and Devan," said Trent, though his expression had hardened.

Hudson took a deep breath and then met Liberty's eyes, who nodded her approval. "That giant wreck over there isn't the only alien ship on this planet," Hudson said to Trent.

Trent's eyebrows raised even higher. "So, where is the other one?"

Hudson looked at Liberty again, and this time she took the lead, "Well, here's the thing, commodore; it sort of took off and flew away..."

CHAPTER 28

Commodore Trent had listened attentively while Hudson and Liberty detailed their discovery of the alien shuttle, and its subsequent disappearance. He had interrupted only when necessary, to clarify key points or ask pertinent questions. And he'd displayed no emotion, other than sometimes being unable to contain his amazement. But he'd also been unable to fully mask his skepticism. Hudson didn't blame him for having some misgivings about their story. After all, in dozens of discovered worlds and wrecks, no-one had ever encountered an alien shuttle before, let alone an active ship. If a stranger had told Hudson the same story, he doubted he would have believed it either.

They had parted ways with Commodore Trent's assurance that he would investigate and take the matter seriously. This alone had both reassured

Hudson, and made him feel a little less guilty about his part in the alien shuttle's reactivation. The alien vessel's intentions were still unknown – in fact, since it had sped out of sight, nothing more had been seen of it at all. But on top of the mysterious, moving red chevron on Liberty's scendar device, he couldn't shake the feeling that it was bad news. Or, at the very least, that it was the harbinger of something dark, looming just over the horizon.

"We have just over three minutes until the deceleration burn is complete," said Hudson, poking his head into the Orion's living space. Liberty was just finishing cataloging their score from the wreck. She'd also separated the relics into the items they would auction on Brahms Three, and the ones they'd store at the Landing Strip with Ma. Liberty acknowledged Hudson's statement, stowed the last of the items into the storage compartments, and followed him back along the connecting corridor to the cockpit.

"How's it looking out there?" asked Liberty, as she slid into the second seat and fastened her harness.

"Take a look for yourself," replied Hudson, indicating to the navigation scanner.

Liberty checked her own panel and saw twenty ships, seemingly looming in orbit above Brahms Three. "I'm guessing a planet like this doesn't normally have so much traffic parked above it?"

she asked, though she already suspected she knew the answer.

"I've never seen Brahms Three's orbit this busy," replied Hudson. "There aren't any orbital stations or facilities, even at the portal. So, you're either arriving or getting the hell away from here as fast as possible. There's no reason to sit in orbit unless you're waiting for something."

"Or someone..." added Liberty. "Once we sell off some of this score, we're going to need to make some serious upgrades to the Orion."

Hudson nodded. "We have to make it down to the scavenger town first."

Liberty looked over at him and smiled, "Best get ready to do some fancy flying, and earn your crust then, Hudson Powell."

Hudson threw up a casual salute, "Yes, sir, co-captain sir!"

Liberty laughed, but then one of her panels bleeped. She checked it, frowning. "There it is again," she said, shaking her head.

"The ghost?" asked Hudson. During their journey back from the planet that Commodore Trent had since named 'Zimmer One', Liberty had periodically picked up what seemed to be a ship on their tail. It would appear a few hundred meters directly astern, but then disappear again. Hudson had even spun the ship around in an attempt to visually scan behind them. However, on every occasion, there was no sign of anything other than black space. The only confirmed contacts had been ships travelling in the opposite direction, to the newly discovered portal world. These had been a combination of CET and RGF colonization assets, plus a raft of impatient hunters, looking to make their fortunes on the new wreck. These eager ships would later camp out beyond the checkpoint perimeter. They'd then wait for the RGF to give the green light for relic hunting operations to begin. Hudson had explained to a fascinated Liberty that this was actually how the first scavenger towns had formed. They'd built up around the tent cities that had sprung up to accommodate the waiting relic hunter crews.

"Yes, it's back again," said Liberty, punching commands into her console. "I'm going to have to strip the control systems for the aft navigational sensors when we get on the ground. It has to be a glitch."

Hudson grabbed the controls and placed his hand on the thruster lever. "We have a blockade to run first..." he said, staring out of the cockpit glass.

Liberty looked up to see a small fleet of ships directly in their flight path to the planet. They were all private vessels, a mix of small, two-person patrols and escorts, up to larger, mid-sized light freighters. "Relic hunters..." said Liberty, exhaling the words as an exasperated sigh.

"Commodore Trent was right; we have suddenly become *very* popular," said Hudson. The registry

IDs of each of the ships started to populate on his panel. Hudson watched anxiously, hoping the one ID he didn't want to see was missing. He then closed his eyes and let out a frustrated sigh. FS-31 Patrol Craft, Hawk-1333F was one of the twenty ships waiting for them. He doubted that Cutler would try to gun them down in front of nineteen witnesses. Still, if things did get heated, there was always a chance he could take a pot shot and get away with it.

"We're getting a flood of messages from the mini armada out there," said Liberty. "They're all variations on a theme. The theme being a demand that we share the method of detecting new portals." Then she rocked her head back and let out a growl that told Hudson she'd just seen what he had seen. "I take it you know that your best friend, Cutler Wendell, is out there too?"

"Unfortunately, I am aware," replied Hudson, though Cutler wasn't at the front of his mind at that moment. He was trying to work out how to break through the blockade and make re-entry over the scavenger town, without getting shot up in the process. The communications panel bleeped, but Hudson ignored it.

"Guess who's calling?" said Liberty.

"Can you take a message? I'm a little busy right now," replied Hudson. He had been joking, but to his surprise, Liberty actually opened a channel.

"M7070-Orion, how may I direct your call?" said Liberty, adopting the voice of a nineteen-fifties switchboard operator.

"Tell me how you found that portal, and I'll stop hunting you," said the voice of Cutler Wendell, crackling over the channel. "This is a one-time offer. I suggest you take it."

"I'm sorry, I think you must have mis-dialed," Liberty continued, still in character, "because nobody at this number gives a shit what you want."

"Just put Powell on, girl," growled Cutler, "I don't have time for your games."

Hudson slid his headset over his ears and opened the mic. "She's trying to give you a hint, asshole. Which, in case you hadn't understood it the first time, was to piss off."

"You're making a mistake," said Cutler, intoning each word with the enthusiasm of an undertaker conducting a funeral service. Then the channel abruptly clicked off.

"I really hate that guy," said Liberty. "Once we upgrade the Orion with weapons, we and Cutler Wendell are going to have a very different kind of conversation."

"Hold that thought until we get on the ground," said Hudson. "And hold onto your seat too; this might get a little sporty..."

Hudson aimed the nose of the Orion at a gap in the blockade and them rammed the throttle forward. The ship surged ahead with a ferocious burst of acceleration which pressed them back into their seats. Had he got the angle even fractionally wrong, he would have accelerated the ship directly on a collision course with one of the other hunters. However, within seconds they'd slipped through, and were soaring on towards the planet.

"That was easy..." said Liberty, fighting against the pressure on her chest to get the words out.

"We're not out of danger yet," replied Hudson, though he was straining to get the words out too. "We'll have to slow down again for entry, and when we do, they'll be on top of us."

Hudson held the five-g burst for a few seconds longer and then rotated the main engine pods, in readiness for their deceleration. Checking the scanner, he could see that some of the other ships had matched or even exceeded his burn. He would be able to make re-entry first, but then the real chase would be on. Some of the hunters would break off, but he knew Cutler, at least, would not. And this meant he'd have to evade them inside Brahms Three's sticky atmosphere long enough for the CET to intervene.

"Throttling back now," said Hudson, expertly killing the bulk of their forward velocity just before the Kármán line – the point beyond which atmospheric entry began.

"Six of the other hunters are still with us," said Liberty, "including Cutler."

"Well, that improves our odds a little at least," said Hudson. Six was certainly better than twenty, but there was only one pursuing ship that he was really worried about. "Get ready for some chop; I'm going in hot."

"Not too hot, I hope!" cried Liberty, gripping the arms of her seat tightly, as the noise in the cabin rose to a roar.

Soon the Orion had left the void of space and penetrated the sweaty, hot atmosphere of Brahms Three. Hudson quickly reconfigured the flight systems for atmospheric flight and then dove the ship rapidly towards the surface.

"I'm going to try to lose them in the valleys out west of the scavenger town," said Hudson. "Keep an eye out for CET patrols. Once we're within a hundred kilometers of the checkpoint district, they should start to take a lot of interest in us."

Hudson dropped the Orion to just thirty meters off the ground, and immediately five of the remaining ships broke off. Hudson smiled, "Chasing us isn't worth them crashing and burning," he said to Liberty, who did not appear to be enjoying Hudson's display of low-flying expertise. "Besides, they need us alive in order to coerce the secrets from us."

"Right now, I'll tell you any secret you want, just to get you to stop!" cried Liberty.

"Tempting..." said Hudson, quickly checking the navigation scanner, and noting the ID of the lone ship still in pursuit. "But we still have Cutler Wendell on our tail."

Hudson continued to weave through the deep valley system that stretched out for thousands of kilometers, beyond the scavenger town. Cutler's ship matched them, move for move. *Damn, that guy can fly* he thought, skimming so close to one hill that the engine exhaust scorched the grass black. Then an alarm rang out. "Hold on!" he cried, banking sharply to port. Tracer fire flashed past his window and slammed into the rolling hills of the valley. He glanced over to Liberty, who was pressed into the seat as if glued to it. "Hang in there, Liberty, we're almost inside the checkpoint perimeter."

Suddenly the ship began to shudder violently. Red lights flashed up across a dozen panels and alerts rang out continuously. Hudson wrestled with the controls, but they were responding sloppily, and then he saw that he was losing thrust.

"Engine two is hit!" cried Liberty. "And we've got damage along the port side flight controls."

If he'd had more altitude, Hudson might have been able to coax the Orion down, but he was already flying too low and too fast. He only had a single option, and it wasn't a good one.

"I'm going to have to crash-land," said Hudson, pulling out of the valley with the little power he had left.

"What?!" cried Liberty. "We'll be sitting ducks!"

"We're going down either way, Liberty," said Hudson, aiming for an open plain, covered in a thick blanket of yellow foliage. "Hang on!"

Hudson pulled up and fired the ventral thrusters in an attempt to kill as much of their downward momentum as possible. Hudson's experience and pilot's instincts paid off, but the Orion still hit the ground solidly, before beginning to carve a furrow through the dense vegetation. The tough, vine-like plants wrapped themselves around the hull like tentacles. It was as if the ship was being wrestled to a stop by a monstrous Kraken.

Hudson unclipped his harness and sprang out from his seat. "Come on, we need to get off the ship, before Cutler comes back to finish us off."

Liberty didn't need telling twice, and together they raced along the corridor into their living space and then out towards the cargo hold. Hudson slammed the emergency ramp release, and the hot, moist air of Brahms Three rushed inside. "Go, go, go!" cried Hudson, urging Liberty out first. Then he raced after her into the furrow carved out by the ship as it had ground to a halt. He was about to call out to Liberty to run into the denser vegetation to hide, but it was too late. Hovering above them was the FS-31 Patrol Craft, belonging to Cutler Wendell. It was so close that Hudson could see the occupants through the oval-shaped cockpit glass. Cutler Wendell was sitting in the second seat, and Tory Bellona was piloting.

"You should have taken my offer, when you had the chance," said Cutler, over an external speaker. Despite his level tone, the delight at having them cornered was still palpable in his voice. "Now, I'll take what I need from your ship. And you can die here, in the dirt, where you belong."

The rotary cannon on the nose of the ship swung down and pointed at them. Hudson knew he'd run out of moves; this time Cutler Wendell had them.

"I'm sorry, Liberty," said Hudson, turning to face his partner. He didn't know what else to say; any other words would be meaningless, he realized.

Hudson knew Liberty had chosen to become a hunter, just as he had. And she had accepted the risks, the same as he had. Equal risk, equal reward. However, he couldn't help but feel the stab of guilt and shame that he hadn't managed to keep them both safe.

Liberty wrapped her arms around him and turned her head away from the cannon, burying it in his chest. Then she spoke three words in reply. "I'm sorry too."

CHAPTER 29

The cannon whirred, but Hudson saw the bullets cut through the ground to their side. He peered back up at Cutler's FS-31 and saw that its nose had suddenly angled away from them.

"Tory, what the hell?!" he heard Cutler cry out through the speaker, before it was abruptly closed off.

Hudson's reaction had been the same as his enemy's. He was used to Tory finding ways to spare them, but on this occasion, he didn't know how she would justify it. A blast of air then hit them from behind, and Hudson and Liberty staggered forward, still holding onto each other for support. Shielding his eyes, he looked back to see a CET military tiltrotor patrol craft hovering above them.

Hudson and Liberty watched in shocked silence as Cutler's ship veered away and then started to climb sharply.

"They're leaving?" said Liberty, sounding more astonished than relieved. Hudson could scarcely believe it himself.

"They can't shoot us in front of the CET," said Hudson, "Not unless they want to spend the rest of their lives in a penal station."

Hudson continued to watch until Cutler's ship had vanished from sight, still barely believing their luck. Then he turned back to the CET vessel as it slowly set down in front of them.

"Maybe that's why Tory turned their cannon away?" suggested Liberty. "Perhaps she saw the CET ship approaching, and stopped Cutler from murdering us in plain sight of them?"

"I don't know, Liberty," said Hudson, managing a weak smile. "But, like her or not, she's saved our asses again."

Liberty scowled, "She was flying the damn ship that shot us down, Hudson," she pointed out.

Hudson couldn't deny that Liberty had a point, but he didn't believe Tory had acted merely to save her own skin. He was now more convinced than ever that the mercenary was still looking out for him, even if her methods weren't always obvious. Maybe he was just believing what he wanted to believe, Hudson admitted, trying to play devil's advocate with himself. However, he was finding it harder and harder to consider Tory Bellona as a threat, or as an enemy.

The side door of the tiltrotor craft slid open and a female officer jumped out and ran towards them. She was wearing what looked like a compact respirator, which covered her face below the nose. Hudson found this odd, considering that Brahms Three wasn't a dusty planet.

The officer then looked at Hudson and Liberty in turn. "Captain Powell, Captain Devan?" she said, shouting over the noise of the twin rotors. With the respirator still covering her face, she sounded like some sort of evil robot. Hudson nodded, and the woman saluted, sharply. "I'm Lieutenant Thorn. Commodore Trent gave orders that I should escort you safely to the scavenger town. Sorry we're a bit late."

Hudson laughed, "On the contrary, you were just in time."

"I'm afraid we weren't able to observe who shot you down," Thorn went on. "The banks of the valley obscured our view. But we just saw that FS-31 check its cannon, so I'm guessing it was them?"

"We've had our differences, put it that way," replied Hudson.

Thorn nodded. "They'll be fined heavily for the unauthorized weapon discharge, and banned from returning to Brahms Three. Beyond that, I'm afraid we can't do any more."

"Thanks, Lieutenant, but they're our problem," said Hudson. "We'll deal with them."

Liberty stepped forward and took a closer look at the tiltrotor. "Nice ship," she said to Thorn, "How much can it lift?"

Thorn seemed pleased at the praise for her vessel. "We use her mainly to move containers around, and haul off the larger hunks of hull from the wrecks."

"Do you think she can haul our ship here back to the spaceport?" asked Liberty.

Thorn took a look at the Orion, its damaged engine still sending a plume of acrid smoke into the air. "Sure, piece of cake. I'll get it hooked up and we'll have you back in no time."

Hudson and Liberty thanked Lieutenant Thorn and backed away. Then Thorn's crew piled out of the tiltrotor and started to hook up chains to the Orion's hull.

Liberty suddenly burst out laughing, and Hudson looked at her, also smirking for some unknown reason. "What's so damn funny?" he asked, but then let out a little chortle himself.

"I don't know," said Liberty, throwing her arms out wide and laughing again. "I should feel like crying, especially after what that bastard did to our ship. But I feel great!"

"So do I!" agreed Hudson, laughing freely this time. Then he nudged her on the shoulder and said, "Hey, we nearly died. Again!" There was a brief silence and then they both exploded into fits of giggles.

Hudson watched as the crew from the tiltrotor ran past, looking at them as if they were mad. "Why are they all wearing respirators?" wondered Liberty, before pointing and laughing at them.

Hudson stifled a chuckle, but then frowned as he looked at the crumpled plants beneath their feet. He reached down and picked up a yellow flower from one of the squashed vines. "Oh dear, this thing is a powerful narcotic," he said, holding out the flower to Liberty, and then laughing again. "Someone tried to sell you a bag in the scavenger town, remember?"

Liberty took the flower and pushed the stem behind her ear. "Pretty," she said, locking eyes with Hudson and trying to keep a straight face. Then they exploded into laughter again, and fell to the ground, holding each other for support. Hudson felt like his ribs were going to break out from his body.

Struggling to their knees, they both watched as the tiltrotor began to hover over the Orion, taking the strain.

"We'd better get back inside," said Hudson, wiping tears from his eyes.

"Whatever you say, skipper," replied Liberty, hauling herself up and then staggering towards the Orion. Suddenly, she stopped and turned back to Hudson. "I'm going to break every bone in Cutler Wendell's weaselly body!" she said, laughing as if she'd just confessed an embarrassing secret.

Hudson rested an arm over her shoulder and together they ambled back into the cargo hold of the Orion. "I've got a serious crush on Tory Bellona!" said Hudson, before pausing and adding, a little more guiltily. "I think it's hot that she keeps hunting me, like a wildcat." Then there was a second of silence, before they burst out laughing again.

Hudson hit the button to close the ramp and they felt the Orion lift into the air. They both lay on their backs on the deck of the cargo hold, trying to catch their breath.

"Hey, Hudson... are we going to be okay?" asked Liberty, suddenly becoming more somber. Now that they were sealed inside the filtered environment of the ship, they were isolated from the powerful effects of the flower.

Hudson looked at her and smiled. He had also felt the drug-induced euphoria subside a little. However, despite their extremely close-call, he was still hopeful. "Yes, Liberty, we're going to be just fine," he told her. "And don't worry about the ship. The Orion will rise again." Then he tapped her on the shoulder with his fist, and held her eyes more intensely. "And so will we; even stronger than before."

CHAPTER 30

M a topped up their tumblers again and then wiped a mirthful tear from her eye. "Trust you to crash-land in a field full of eupha poppies," said Ma, still laughing at the crazy story of how they'd arrived back at Brahms Three. "You two had better hope that you're cats, considering how quickly you're burning through lives."

"Yeah, well the next time some asshole takes a pot-shot at us, we'll be able to respond in kind," replied Hudson, taking a swig of his beer. Then he raised the bottle to Ma and added, "Thanks for hooking us up with Dean's Ship Services, by the way."

Dean's Ship Services sounded – and looked – like a mundane, and slightly dodgy, starship repair shop. However, it was actually much more. Ma's many years as a relic hunter had furnished her with a number of shady underworld contacts, and the eponymous Dean was one of them. In addition to repairing the Orion's damaged engine and flight controls, Dean had outfitted the tough little ship with a number of major upgrades. This included concealable weapons, comprising a ventral machine gun on a 360-degree mount, and a 30mm cannon in the nose. The latter was pulled from a decommissioned CET Corvette, and packed enough of a punch to take on ships three times the Orion's size. Dean had also forged new alloy armor plating using some of the alien metal they'd recovered from the wreck on Zimmer One. The extensive repairs and upgrades hadn't been cheap, costing them most of what they'd recovered from the wreck. But they still had enough to pay Ma's storage fees, and keep a little in reserve as a rainy-day fund.

"I'm itching to take her out again," said Liberty, sipping her beer. "With the upgrades to the engines and thrusters, she should fly even harder than before."

Ma's Immaculately-plucked eyebrows raised up. "Are you sure you don't just want to have a nice, safe hunt on the wreck here?"

Liberty looked at Hudson, who smiled back, before they both said in unison, "Nah."

"You two are gluttons for punishment," replied Ma, shaking her head. Then her expression softened, and her normally discriminating eyes appeared more philosophical. "Though, I don't blame you. If I had this magic crystal of yours, I'd be off exploring new portal worlds too." Ma raised her glass of whiskey and downed the contents. "Unfortunately, I'm not as young as Liberty here. My hunting days are done."

"Hey, I'm still young too you know," complained Hudson. "Besides, you could still wrangle with the best of them, if you wanted to, Ma."

Ma reached over and slapped Hudson's face affectionately, though because of her strength it felt more like an assault.

Hudson noticed that Liberty seemed to have zoned out, and was staring over into the far corner of the bar. He followed the line of her gaze and saw a single figure, sitting at the corner table. The other patrons were all the regulars Hudson remembered from the last time they'd frequented the Landing Strip.

"What are you thinking, Liberty?" asked Hudson, turning back to his partner.

"I'm not sure," replied Liberty, and then she looked up at Ma. "Who is the person in the corner over there?"

Ma glanced over briefly and then shrugged. "Just some random guy. Came in shortly after the first time you two dropped off the relics for storage."

Hudson thought back, remembering that they'd only briefly popped into the Landing Strip after the CET tiltrotar had deposited the Orion in the spaceport. It had been a fleeting visit, simply to stash their remaining relics. They'd then gone to Dean's Ship Services to order the repairs and upgrades, before returning to have the drink they were all enjoying now.

"Could he have followed us here?" said Liberty, more to Hudson than to Ma, but it was Ma that replied.

"He seems harmless enough," said Ma. "No weapons, unless he's concealing them very well. Keeps buying drinks, so I'm happy." Then she seemed to remember something. "Though it was damned odd the first time he came in. He didn't have a hardbuck to his name, and seemed not even to know what I was talking about. But then he left and came back ten minutes later with a whole stack of cash."

"That is odd," said Hudson, glancing back over at the man.

"I don't care where he got it from, so long as he didn't steal it from anyone I like," said Ma. And then with more than a twinkle in her eye she added. "But since I don't like most folk, I doubt that's likely."

Hudson necked his shot and then chased it with the last of his beer. "I think we should be getting back to the ship," he said, raising an eyebrow at Liberty. The Landing Strip was a safe haven, but they still had to walk through the scavenger town to get back to the Orion. And that would leave them temporarily exposed and vulnerable. He didn't want to let it get too late before they headed back.

"I'll put this on your tab," said Ma, clearing away the glasses. "And I look forward to seeing what other new relics you two dig up from the next virgin wreck you find."

"Except next time, we'll hopefully be able to bring them back, without getting shot down," said Liberty. She then finished her beer, and slid the empty bottle to Ma.

They said their goodbyes, then Hudson and Liberty left, walking out into the scavenger town. It was still peak time for the bars and clubs, so the streets were busy. Nevertheless, Hudson hurried, encouraging Liberty to move quickly too.

"Keep an eye out behind us, Liberty," said Hudson, "I've got a bad feeling about that guy in the bar."

"I know what you mean," replied Liberty, quickly glancing behind. "I never thought being famous would turn out to be so dangerous."

They hurried on through the streets, brushing off the pimps and pushers, until they reached the spaceport. Liberty used the Orion's ID fob to enter the compound, while Hudson watched their rear. His hand was inside his leather jacket, clasped around the grip of the pistol, just in case of trouble.

"I know you hate weapons, but you really need to think about arming yourself," Hudson said, feeling his pulse thumping in his neck.

The gate unlocked and Liberty pushed through, holding it open for Hudson. "I'm not getting a pistol or some crazy revolver like your girlfriend has," said Liberty, drawing a withered look from Hudson. "But I'll think about what else I can carry."

"Good enough," replied Hudson, slamming the gate shut, and waiting for the lock to activate again. He heard the comforting thud of the bolt and let out a relieved sigh. "We're in the clear. Now, let's get on-board and seal her up tight. I've had enough excitement for one day."

"I hear you…" said Liberty. She lowered the rear ramp and they both climbed up into the cargo hold, and waited for it to whir shut again.

Hudson slapped Liberty gently on the back as he led the way up to the living quarters. "Come on, there's a bottle of Ma's whiskey waiting for us." He climbed the stairs and opened the door into the living space, but then froze. Sitting quietly on the semi-circular couch was the man from the Landing Strip.

CHAPTER 31

Hudson reached inside his jacket and drew the pistol, before aiming it at the stranger. "What are you doing here?" he demanded, as Liberty moved through, spotted the intruder, and froze. "Who are you? Explain yourself!"

The man rose slowly and stepped out in front of them. Hudson watched him closely, ready to fire should he show the slightest hint of aggression.

"Has Goliath returned?" the man asked. His voice was stilted, as if English was not his native language.

"Who the hell is Goliath?" demanded Hudson. Now that he saw the man more closely, his skin seemed to have a glossy sheen to it, as if covered in a thin layer of grease. And his clothes appeared completely seamless, as if he'd been sewn tightly into them.

"Is System 5118208 still viable?" the man asked, ignoring Hudson's question.

"Look, I don't know any Goliath, and I don't know what system five one one... whatever is either," Hudson replied. "Now you answer my questions, or the next response I'll give you is a bullet from this pistol." Hudson had no intention of shooting the man in cold blood, but he felt his 'tough guy' relic hunter persona was justified.

"Your words cannot explain what I am," the man said. "To use a blend of terms you understand, the best fit would be that I am a Revocater pilot."

"I don't know what that is, and I'm rapidly losing patience," Hudson snapped back.

"I am here to learn if Goliath has returned," the man continued. "You reactivated me. Your ship carries the signal. These are the answers to your questions."

"I reactivated you?" repeated Hudson, who was now genuinely losing his cool, and not just putting on a show of it. "What the hell does that even mean?"

Then Liberty cut in. "The ship, on Zimmer One? That was you?"

"Correct, I was the ship at System 2691313518. The planet your species recently designated, Zimmer One," said the man.

"You followed us back?" said Liberty, and then she seemed to have an epiphany. "You were the ghost."

"I was not a fictitious ethereal entity," said the man, appearing to look confused, though his expression was as alien-looking as the rest of him. "But I did conceal my pursuit. You should not have been able to detect me. It suggests that you possess what your words would describe as, 'the crystal', and that you have harnessed its power."

Hudson was annoyed that Liberty seemed to be more fascinated with the intruder than threatened by or afraid of him. "Look, I don't care what you claim to be – you broke onto our ship, and you need to leave." The man took a step forward, and Hudson straightened his arm, aiming squarely at the intruder's chest. "Don't come any closer," he warned. "I don't want to use this, but I will if I have to."

The man frowned again. "You appear to be highly threatened by this form. Perhaps another would assist with reducing your levels of cortisol, adrenaline and norepinephrine." Then the man changed shape in front of their eyes. First the figure became featureless and smooth, taking on an almost liquid, shimmering golden color. Then it morphed into the form of a woman. Hudson couldn't believe what he'd seen; the man was now a woman, and even more bizarrely she looked like Liberty. Hudson glanced over at his partner, who now looked like she'd seen a real ghost, before again confronting the intruder.

"What the hell are you?" he yelled. "No tricks this time!"

"Does this form not ease your anxiety?" said the woman. Then she changed again, becoming an amorphous shimmering mass, before adopting the form of Ma. "How about this form? This human female elicits feelings of trust from you."

"Enough already!" cried Hudson, "You need to get out, now!"

The woman looked quizzically at Hudson, but then its expression flattened again. "Very well, I will leave and return when your stress hormones have lowered to a more manageable level."

The woman moved slowly around the side of the room, while Hudson and Liberty circled in the opposite direction. The alien then morphed back into its original male form and stopped at the door leading out into the cargo hold.

"I must discover if Goliath is returning," he said. "Goliath will destroy System 5118208, and any other planets that have since harbored sentient life. It will eradicate the corporeal seed-species your words describe as humans, unless it can be stopped."

The intruder turned and moved through the door, but Liberty dashed forward. "Wait!" she called out, and the man turned back to face her. "System 5118208. What is that?"

The man's eyes widened slightly. "It is the collection of planetary bodies you know as the solar system. Goliath's final target was the planet you call Earth." Then he turned and disappeared through the door.

Hudson and Liberty remained in stunned silence for several seconds, before the realization of what had been said hit them like a sledgehammer. Liberty ran after the man first, but Hudson was only a heartbeat behind. He had thought the alien shuttle was the threat, but it had actually come to warn them of the real danger. And they had let it walk out of the door, before finding out who it really was, and what it planned to do. However, when they reached the balcony overlooking the cargo hold, the rear ramp was still sealed shut, and the mysterious, shape-shifting alien was nowhere to be seen.

CHAPTER 32

Liberty poured Hudson a measure of whiskey from Ma's signature, square bottle, and then topped up her own glass. They had both already downed two shots while sitting in silence on their semi-circular couch in the living space. The only question each had posed to the other was what to do next. However, in light of what had just happened, they were both completely flummoxed.

What just happened? Hudson asked himself again. *Did we just meet with an alien species? An alien AI? A shape-shifting alien AI?* However he sliced it, the answer was simply fantastical, and unbelievable. Yet he'd seen the man change into a woman in front of his very eyes. Twice, in fact – and then back to a man again. He realized that he'd had a few drinks at the Landing Strip, but not enough to create that level of hallucination. And the effects of the eupha poppy had worn off long

257

ago. The only conclusion was that what they'd experienced was real, and as such could not be ignored.

"I'll send an encoded message to Commodore Trent, letting him know that the alien from Zimmer One made contact," said Hudson, after taking a sip of the whiskey.

"He'll think we've gone mad," replied Liberty. "Or madder... I think he already believes we have a bolt or two loose."

"I'm starting to think he might be right," said Hudson. "But this is too big for just the two of us. If this truly is an alien intelligence that is somehow linked to the wrecks, then the implications are..." Hudson paused and shrugged, unable to articulate the enormity of the event, before settling on, "well, bigger than anything I can imagine."

"What do you think this Goliath is?" asked Liberty, taking a tiny sip of her drink. From the attempted nonchalance with which she'd asked the question, Hudson could tell it was something that had been playing on her mind. "Morphus said its final target was Earth."

"Morphus?" repeated Hudson, frowning.

"That's what I've decided to call our shape-shifting alien invader," replied Liberty. "I think it has a nice ring to it, don't you?"

"I think giving it a name is the least of our concerns, but I guess Morphus is as good as any," replied Hudson, managing a smile. "As to your question, I honestly don't want to think about it. But whatever this Goliath is, it doesn't sound good. Ultimately, only our friend Morphus can give us a concrete answer."

Liberty nodded. "He, she, it... did say he would come back. Maybe we should just hang around on Brahms Three until he returns."

Hudson thought about this for a moment and then let out a pensive sigh. "Judging by how easily he managed to track us back here, and get into the ship, I don't think it will struggle to find us again." Then he finished the rest of his whiskey and added, "I say we carry on as if nothing happened, and just wait and see."

Liberty nodded, "Okay, so where do we head to next?"

Hudson smiled and slid out from the couch. "I seem to remember someone wanting to see Mars?"

"That would be me!" said Liberty, the prospect of a visit to the red planet destroying any trace of anxiety.

Hudson set off towards the cockpit. "There are a few ways to get there, but the quickest is to hop back through the portal to Chopin Four, and then cut across to Minerva Three, in MP territory. From there, it's one hop back to Mars. It will be quicker than heading back to Earth and then making the transit from there."

"I don't mind," said Liberty. "It would be good to get some R&R, so a few days of interstellar travel doesn't bother me."

Hudson entered the cockpit with Liberty just behind, and then slid into his seat. "Let's just see which way the wind blows us then," he said, powering up the main engines. The pitch of their whine was different to what he remembered. Then he recalled that Dean of Dean's Ship Services had given them a hefty tune-up. "It will be fun to see what I can do with the newly upgraded Orion."

Liberty fastened her harness, but then peeked over at him with a sly smile. "So long as what you do is not crash it again, then I'm all good."

Hudson was about to protest, but then he saw Liberty's cheeky grin, and relaxed. "How about you get us clearance to leave, instead of giving me grief?"

"Whatever you say, skipper," replied Liberty, sliding on her headset and calling up the control tower.

As soon as they received clearance to leave, Hudson lifted the Orion up above the decadent scavenger town of Brahms Three. He circled around the town, spotting Ma's bar amongst the mass of converted shipping containers, and then powered the Orion into orbit. Thanks to the newly-upgraded engines, progress was swift, and Hudson again marveled at how well screwed together the nimble VCX-110 was. However, it wasn't long after they'd left the atmosphere of the planet, before Hudson noticed that they weren't alone.

"It looks like we've acquired an entourage..." said Hudson, pointing to the navigation scanner.

Liberty checked it and laughed. "So long as they don't all try to shoot us down, let them follow."

Hudson adjusted course to the portal and accelerated harder, hoping to shake off some of the smaller, slower ships. However, as they approached the portal and he began their deceleration burn, Hudson noticed that the convoy hadn't reduced in number. "Perhaps taking the long way around from Earth is the better option," said Hudson. "A lot of these ships aren't built for longer interplanetary journeys. They'll break off once they realize where we're headed."

Liberty didn't answer. Instead she was busily checking her screens, her brow furrowed in what Hudson recognized to be her 'concerned frown'. "What's up?" he said, hoping the answer didn't start with 'Cutler' and end with 'Wendell'.

"There's a ship heading for us from the portal," said Liberty, "It's putting itself directly in our flight path."

"Let me guess... FS-31 Patrol Craft Hawk-1333F?" said Hudson, with a sinking feeling. However, to his surprise Liberty shook her head.

"For once, no," replied Liberty. "It is another relic hunter, though."

Hudson sucked in his bottom lip and pushed the Orion into a higher approach to the portal, by pulsing the ventral thrusters. The hunter ship matched his maneuver, ensuring that they were still on a collision course. It was now only a kilometer away, and Hudson decided to reduce speed to ensure they didn't plough straight through it.

"There's a message coming through from the ship," said Liberty. "He says his name is Rex, and that you owe him."

"Rex?" repeated Hudson; the name rang a bell, and then he remembered, and huffed a laugh. Rex was the relic hunter that he'd tangled with inside the wreck on Brahms Three. He evidently still blamed him for Tory Bellona getting the better of him and his sons, despite the fact Hudson had essentially saved the brawny man's life.

"Something funny?" said Liberty.

"Only that relic hunters seem to like holding grudges," replied Hudson.

Liberty scowled, but didn't press Hudson to elaborate on his vague answer. "Well, Mr. Grudge is demanding that we turn over whatever device we have that detects portals, otherwise he'll start shooting."

"Oh, really?" said Hudson. He was tired of people threatening him, and in no mood for games. "I think you know exactly how to respond to that request, don't you, co-captain Devan?"

Liberty smiled. "Yes, indeed I do, co-captain Powell..."

Then Liberty pulled a control stick towards her – a new addition to the cockpit – and entered a sequence of commands. Seconds later, gears whirred deep inside the ship as the ventral turret-mounted machine gun and 30mm nose cannon slid out of their secret concealed locations. Liberty grabbed the control stick and a targeting reticule appeared overlaid on the cockpit glass. The other relic hunter vessel now loomed large in front of them. It was a bigger, but older and clunkier modified freighter. Liberty aimed just above the bubble of glass where the cockpit was located and squeezed the trigger. A chainsaw buzz rattled through the deck plating and a stream of bullets streaked just over the top of the freighter. A second later, the ship hurriedly veered away and engaged its main engines.

"Do you think they got the message?" asked Hudson, smiling.

"If the message was, 'we're not taking any shit from anyone' then, yes, I think they got it loud and clear."

They both laughed and then Liberty stowed their secret armament again, before Hudson maneuvered them towards the portal. There had been a short queue of ships waiting to make the jump, but as the Orion approached, they all peeled away. It was like a pack of wolves showing deference to an Alpha. The message had been heard loud and clear, and not only by Rex. Everyone now knew that the Orion was not a ship to be messed with.

CHAPTER 33

Thanks to Liberty's skill at re-starting the engines after a portal transition, it had been smooth sailing after leaving Brahms Three. And while some of their convoy had remained, all but two had given up the pursuit when it became clear that the Orion was heading deeper into the solar system.

Hudson locked in the autopilot and kept the thrust at a standard one-g, before unclipping his harness. "I don't know about you, but I'm beat," he said, running a hand through his hair. "I'm going to try to sleep as much of this trip away as I can."

Then he glanced over at Liberty and noticed she was smiling. He was glad to see that she was still in good spirits, despite the mortal dangers they had faced over the last few days. He'd always thought she was tough, but she'd proven tougher than he had ever imagined. And, if he was honest, she'd probably coped better than he had in some situations. He was glad to have her at his side, even if it sometimes felt like having a partner only doubled his worries. However, it could also help spread the burden too, Hudson realized. This was something he needed to remind himself of more often than he did.

"Something funny in today's epaper?" asked Hudson, curious to learn why Liberty was smiling.

"I'm not looking at the epaper," said Liberty, pointing to the screen. Hudson stepped beside her and saw that she was actually watching the navigation scanner, overlaid with data from her scendar device.

"I know you're a nerd, but finding navigation data amusing is pushing it, even for you..." said Hudson. And then he caught an elbow in his ribs for the trouble.

"It's what the scanner is showing that I'm smiling about," said Liberty. "If you'd look, rather than making wise-ass remarks, you'd see it too."

Hudson leant in closer and then noticed a contact on the scanner, close in behind them. At first, he felt a swell of panic in his gut, jumping to the conclusion it was Cutler Wendell. However, he then realized that Liberty would have alerted him if it was a danger. Also, the shape of the chevron was uniquely different to the other relic-hunter vessels, which were trailing much further behind.

Hudson clicked his fingers, finally putting two and two together.

"Is that Morphus?" said Hudson. Liberty just smiled more broadly and waggled her eyebrows at him.

"I managed to calibrate the scendar device to pick up his ship," said Liberty. "Though how the hell he managed to stay with us this whole time, without being seen, is a mystery."

"Add it to the list..." commented Hudson.

"I actually feel comforted knowing he's still with us," Liberty went on. "I accept that we don't know a damn thing about him, or even if he's friendly. Or even if he's a he, she or it! But I feel somehow safer knowing he's out there." Then she glanced up at Hudson, her eyes seeking reassurance. "Is that weird?"

Hudson shook his head, "Not at all. He may have scared the shit out of me at first, but in truth there was nothing threatening about him."

Liberty pushed up out of her seat and slung an arm around Hudson. "Come on, let's see if we can finish off that bottle of whiskey, before you sleep the rest of the flight to Mars."

"I like your thinking," replied Hudson, before allowing Liberty to lead him towards the living space. "Although, I regret that I may have become a bad influence on you," he added, as he slid onto the semi-circular couch. "When we first met, a few shots of Ma's 'special reserve' would have knocked you on your ass."

Liberty placed two glasses on the table and then filled them from the square bottle, which was just under two-thirds full. "You've certainly had an influence on me, that's for sure," she said, sliding one of the glasses to Hudson. "But despite everything – including the parts where we almost died – I'm happy we did this." Liberty raised her glass, "Thanks for proving me right."

Hudson took his glass and raised it too. "I'm happy we did this too," he replied. And as soon as he'd said the words, Hudson realized that he really meant them too. He'd taken a crazy chance on a stranger he'd only just met, and she had done the same, yet remarkably it had worked out. However, something about the way Liberty had phrased her statement perplexed him a little, and he frowned over at her. "Wait, how did I prove you right?"

"By not turning out to be a complete asshole, of course," replied Liberty, before adding with a darker edge, "...or a serial killer."

Hudson laughed. "Well, thank you for taking a chance on a washed-out old flyer like me."

"You're not old, Hudson Powell," said Liberty, with genuine feeling. "You're just like me. Alive."

Hudson nodded and then chinked his glass against Liberty's. "To the hunt – wherever it may take us."

"To the hunt," Liberty repeated. "And to our next adventure at the red planet of Mars!" Then they both downed the shots, and slammed their glasses down onto the table in perfect synchrony.

The end.

EPILOGUE

Goliath had spent millennia lying dormant, adrift in the unknown reaches of the galaxy. Lost and alone. Though the titanic vessel had slept, it had also dreamed of completing its function. Yet as the years slipped endlessly by, the dream had twisted into a nightmare, taunting it with the disappointment and shame of failure. Now the nightmare had ended. Now it would finally get to complete its task, and allow itself to rest.

As the titanic vessel drew power from the star, feeding its reactors with the energy of creation itself, it thought of nothing but the one planet that escaped its cleansing might. System 5118208. The population of the third planet had been primitive and weak at the time, and barely able to use rudimentary tools. Yet like all organics that had grown from the seed of first sentient corporeals, they possessed the potential to evolve. And like all sentient corporeals, they had to be eliminated. That had not been the function that Goliath's creators had assigned it. However, the great ship had decided that it was the true purpose to its existence. And unlike the corporeals that had bestowed it with life, Goliath would not fail. Goliath would not fall.

The light of the star faded and Goliath moved on, forever searching for the signal that had called to it, like a beacon. With each jump closer, the signal grew stronger and clearer. With each jump, Goliath came closer to its goal.

The energy inside the city-sized generators that lay at the heart of the ship built to a peak. And then Goliath expelled their vitality into space, like blood from an open wound. The portal grew and Goliath slipped through and jumped. It was another step closer to System 5118208. It was another step closer to eradicating all life on Earth.

TO BE CONTINUED

The Star Scavenger Series continues in book three, Goliath Emerges.

Goliath Emerges:

READ THE OTHER BOOKS IN THE SERIES:

- Guardian Outcast
- Orion Rises
- Goliath Emerges
- Union's End
- The Last Revocater

ALSO BY THIS AUTHOR

If you enjoyed this book, please consider reading The Contingency War Series, also by G J Ogden, available from Amazon and free to read for Kindle Unlimited subscribers. Also available as an audiobook on Amazon, Audible and iTunes.

- The Contingency
- The Waystation Gambit
- Rise of Nimrod Fleet
- Earth's Last War

"Highly recommended - sci-fi fans will not be disappointed with this novel."
Readers' Favorite, 5-star review.

No-one comes in peace. Every being in the galaxy wants something, and is willing to take it by force...

ABOUT THE AUTHOR

At school I was asked to write down the jobs I wanted to do as a 'grown up'. Number one was astronaut and number two was a PC games journalist. I only managed to achieve one of those goals (I'll let you guess which), but these two very different career options still neatly sum up my lifelong interests in science, space and the unknown.

School also steered me in the direction of a science-focused education over literature and writing, which influenced my decision to study physics at Manchester University. What this degree taught me is that I didn't like studying physics, and instead enjoyed writing, which is why you're reading this book! The lesson? School can't tell you who you are.

When not writing, I enjoy spending time with my family, walking in the British countryside, and indulging in as much Sci-Fi as possible.

You can connect with me here:
https://twitter.com/GJ_Ogden
www.ogdenmedia.net

Subscribe to my newsletter:
http://subscribe.ogdenmedia.net

Made in the USA
Middletown, DE
15 November 2022

15024831R00168